'So, what keeps you warm in bed at night?'

Zoe flushed. 'I don't think that's any of your damned business. And I thought the point of this lunch was for me to find out about *you*.'

'Ask what you want,' he said. 'I am ready to answer.'

'Well, your second name might be a start.' She tried to sound casual, not easy when her nerves seemed to be stretched on wires.

Oh, what's the matter with me? she wondered savagely. Any other single girl on holiday would relish being chatted up by someone with half his attraction and sheer charisma. Why can't I just—go with the flow?

'My second name is Stephanos,' he said. 'Andreas Stephanos.'

Sara Craven was born in South Devon, and grew up surrounded by books in a house by the sea. After leaving grammar school she worked as a local journalist, covering everything from flower shows to murders. She started writing for Mills & Boon® in 1975. Apart from writing, her passions include films, music, cooking and eating in good restaurants. She now lives in Somerset.

Sara Craven has appeared as a contestant on the Channel Four game show *Fifteen to One* and is also the latest (and last ever) winner of the *Mastermind of Great Britain* championship.

Recent titles by the same author:

THE TOKEN WIFE
THE FORCED MARRIAGE
HIS CONVENIENT MARRIAGE

HIS FORBIDDEN BRIDE

BY
SARA CRAVEN

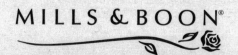

*First published in Great Britain 2003
Harlequin Mills & Boon Limited,
Eton House, 18-24 Paradise Road, Richmond, Surrey TW9 1SR*

© Sara Craven 2003

ISBN 0 263 83308 9

*Set in Times Roman 10½ on 11 pt.
01-0803-54267*

*Printed and bound in Spain
by Litografía Rosés, S.A., Barcelona*

CHAPTER ONE

'I'VE been giving matters a lot of thought,' said George. 'And I feel very strongly that you and I should get married.'

Zoe Lambert, who had just taken a mouthful of Chardonnay, managed by a superhuman effort not to choke to death.

If anyone else had made a similarly preposterous suggestion, she would have laughed them to scorn. But she couldn't do that to George, sitting across from her at the table in the wine bar, with his untidy brown hair, and crooked tie.

George was her friend, one of the few she had at Bishop Cross Sixth Form College, where he was a member of the maths department, and after the weekly staff meeting they usually went for a drink together, but they'd never had a date as such. Nor was there the slightest spark of attraction between them. And even if she'd ever been marginally tempted to fall in love with George, the thought of his mother would have stopped her dead in her tracks.

George's mother was a frail widow with a tungsten core, and she took no prisoners in her bid to keep her son safely at home with her, an obedient and enslaved bachelor. None of George's sporadic romantic interests had ever thrived under the frost of her pale blue gaze, and she planned that none of them ever would. And those steely eyes would narrow to slits if she found out that her only son was in the town's one and only wine bar with Zoe Lambert of all people, let alone proposing marriage.

She took a deep breath. 'George,' she said gently. 'I don't think...'

'After all,' George went on, unheedingly, warming to his

5

theme. 'You're going to find things difficult now that you're—alone. You were so brave all the time your mother was—ill. Now I'd like to look after you. I don't want you to worry any more about anything.'

Except your mother poisoning my food, thought Zoe. Urged on, no doubt, by her best friend, my aunt Megan.

She winced inwardly as she recalled her aunt's chilling demeanour at the funeral two weeks earlier. Megan Arnold had curtly accepted the commiserations from her late sister's friends and neighbours, but had barely addressed a word to the niece who was now her only living relative.

Back at the cottage, after the service, she had refused all offers of food and drink, staring instead, in silent and narrow-eyed appraisal, at her surroundings.

'Never mind, dearie,' Mrs Gibb, who'd cleaned the cottage each week for Gina Lambert over the past ten years, whispered consolingly as she went past a mute and bewildered Zoe with a plate of sandwiches. 'Grief takes some people in funny ways.'

But Zoe could see no evidence of grieving in her aunt's stony face. Megan Arnold had stayed aloof during her younger sister's months of illness. And if she was mourning now, she kept it well hidden. And there'd been no sign of her since the funeral either.

Zoe shook away these unpleasant and uneasy reflections, pushed a strand of dark blonde hair back from her face, and looked steadily at her unexpected suitor with clear grey eyes.

'Are you saying that you've fallen in love with me, George?' she asked mildly.

'Well—I'm very fond of you, Zoe.' He played with the stem of his glass, looking embarrassed. 'And I have the most tremendous respect for you. You must know that. But I don't think I'm the type for this head-over-heels stuff,' he added awkwardly. 'And I suspect you aren't either. I really think it's more important for people to be—friends.'

'Yes,' she said. 'I can understand that. And you could

be right.' *But not about me,* she thought. *Oh, please God, not about me.*

She swallowed. 'George, you're terribly kind, and I do appreciate everything you've said, but I'm not going to make any immediate decisions about the future.' She paused. 'Losing my mother is still too raw, and I'm not seeing things altogether clearly yet.'

'Well, I realise that, naturally.' He reached across the table and patted her hand, swiftly and nervously. 'And I won't put any pressure on you, I swear. I'd just like you to—think about what I've said. Will you do that?'

'Yes,' Zoe told him, mentally crossing her fingers. 'Of course I will.'

My first marriage proposal, she thought. How utterly bizarre.

He was silent for a moment. 'If you did think you could marry me at some point,' he said hesitantly, 'I wouldn't want to—rush you into anything, afterwards. I'd be prepared to wait—as long as you wanted.'

Zoe bit her lip as she looked back at the kind, anxious face. 'George,' she said. 'I truly do not deserve you.' And meant it.

It was hard to think about anything else as the local bus jolted its way through the lanes half an hour later, but she knew she had to try. Because George's extraordinary proposal was only one of her current problems. And possibly the least pressing, bless him.

She had come to Astencombe to share her mother's cottage three years ago when she had left university, and not long before Gina Lambert's condition had first been diagnosed. But the property was only rented. It had belonged to Aunt Megan's late husband, Peter Arnold, and he had agreed the original lease with his sister-in-law.

Zoe suspected this had always been a bone of contention with his wife, and, since his death, Aunt Megan had raised the rent slowly and steadily each year, although as a wealthy and childless widow she could not possibly need the money. She had also insisted that maintenance and repairs were the responsibility of her tenant.

Gina, also a widow, had eked out her husband's meagre company pension with her skill as a landscape artist, but it had been a precarious living, and Zoe's salary as an English teacher had been a welcome addition to the household budget. Particularly when the time had come when her mother had no longer been able to paint.

Finding a local job and living at home was not what she'd planned to do originally, of course. At university she'd met Mick, who'd intended, after graduation, to travel round the world for a year, taking what work he could find to earn his living on the way. He'd wanted her to go with him, and she'd been sorely tempted.

In fact, she'd gone home for the weekend to tell her mother what she meant to do, but had arrived to find Gina oddly quiet, and frail-looking. She had stoutly denied there was anything the matter, but Zoe had soon learned through the village grapevine that Aunt Megan had made one of her periodic descents the day before, and, as Adele who lived next door had put it, 'There'd been words.'

Zoe had spent the whole weekend trying to tell her mother about her plans, and failing. Instead, obeying an instinct she barely understood, she had found herself informing Mick that she'd changed her mind about the trip. She'd hoped against hope that he loved her enough not to want to go without her, but she'd been rudely disappointed.

Mick, she realised with shocked hurt, was not about to change his mind—just his choice of travelling companion. And the love she'd blithely thought was hers for ever had proved a very transient affair instead. Within days she'd been comprehensively replaced in his bed and affections.

But it had taught her a valuable lesson about men, she thought wryly, and maybe it was better to be dumped in England than the middle of the Hindu Kush. Since Mick, she'd had no serious involvement with anyone. And now she'd been proposed to by George, who did not love her either. History, it seemed, was repeating itself.

If I'm not careful, I shall get a complex, she told herself.

Looking back, however, she had no regrets about sacrificing her independence. The job and the village might have their limitations, but she was so thankful that she'd been there for her mother through the initial tests, the hospital treatments, and subsequent brief remission. And through her mercifully short final illness. Even at the last Gina's warmth and optimism had not deserted her, and Zoe had many memories to treasure in spite of her sadness.

But the fact remained that she'd reached the end of a chapter in her life. And she didn't see the rest of her life being devoted to Bishops Cross college. She had the contents of the cottage, and a little money to come from her mother's will as soon as it was proved. Maybe this was her chance to move on, and make a new life for herself.

One thing was certain. Aunt Megan would not be sorry to see the back of her.

How could two sisters be so totally unalike? she wondered sadly. True, her aunt was the elder by twelve years, but there had never seemed to be any sibling feeling between them.

'I think Megan liked being an only child,' Gina had explained ruefully when Zoe had questioned her once on the subject. 'And my arrival was a total embarrassment to her.'

'Did she never want a baby of her own?' Zoe asked.

Gina looked past her, her face oddly frozen. 'At one time, perhaps,' she said. 'But it just—didn't happen for her.' She sighed briefly. 'Poor Megan.'

Megan was taller, too, thinner and darker than her younger sister, with a face that seemed permanently set in lines of resentment. There was no glimpse in her of the underlying joy in living that had characterised Gina, underpinning the occasional moments when she'd seemed to withdraw into herself, trapped in some private and painful world. Her 'quiet times' as she'd called them wryly.

Zoe had wondered sometimes what could possibly prompt them. She could only assume it was memories of her father. Maybe their quiet, apparently uneventful marriage had concealed an intense passion that her mother still mourned.

Her aunt was a very different matter. On the face of it Mrs Arnold seemed to have so much to content her. She'd never had to worry about money in her life, and her husband had been a kind, ebullient man, immensely popular in the locality. The attraction of opposites, Zoe had often thought. There could be no other explanation for such an ill-assorted pairing.

In addition, her aunt had a lovely Georgian house, enclosed behind a high brick wall, from which she emerged mainly to preside over most of the organisations in the area, in a one-woman reign of terror. But not even that seemed to have the power to make her happy.

And her dislike of her younger sister seemed to have passed seamlessly to her only niece. Even the fact that Megan Arnold had once taught English herself had failed to provide a common meeting ground. Zoe couldn't pretend to be happy about her aunt's determined hostility, but she'd learned to offer politeness when they met, and expect nothing in return.

She got off the bus at the crossroads, and began to walk down the lane. It was still a warm, windy day, bringing wafts of hedgerow scents, and Zoe gave a brief sigh of satisfaction as she breathed the fragrant air. Public examinations always made this a difficult term at college, and she might unwind by doing a little work in the garden tonight, she thought as she turned the slight corner that led to home. She'd always found weeding and dead-heading therapeutic, so while she worked she could consider the future as well. Review her options.

And stopped dead, her brows snapping together, as she saw that the front garden of the cottage had acquired a new and unexpected addition. A 'For Sale' board, she registered with a kind of helpless disbelief, with the logo of a local estate agency, had been erected just inside the white picket fence.

It must be a mistake, she thought, covering the last few yards at a run. I'll have to call them.

As she reached the gate, Adele appeared in the neighbouring doorway, her youngest child, limpet-like, on her hip.

'Did you know about that?' she inquired, nodding at the sign. And as Zoe speechlessly shook her head she sighed. 'I thought not. When they came this morning, I queried it, but they said they were acting on the owner's instructions.' She jerked her head towards the cottage. 'She's there now, waiting for you. Just opened the door with her own key and marched in.'

'Oh, hell,' Zoe muttered. 'That's all I need.'

She pulled a ferocious face as she lifted the latch and let herself into the cottage.

She found Megan Arnold in the sitting room, standing in front of the empty fireplace, staring fixedly at the picture that hung above the mantelpiece.

Zoe hesitated in the doorway, watching her, puzzled. It was an unusual painting, quite unlike Gina Lambert's usual choice of subject. It seemed to be a Mediterranean scene— a short flight of white marble steps, scattered with the faded petals of some pink flower, flanked on one side by a plain white wall, and leading up to a terrace with a balustrade. And on the edge of the balustrade, against a background of vivid blue sky and azure sea, a large ornamental urn bright with pelargoniums in pink, crimson and white.

What made it all the more curious was that the Lamberts had always taken their holidays at home, usually in Cornwall, or the Yorkshire Dales. As far as Zoe was aware, the Mediterranean was an unknown quantity to her mother. And it was the only time she'd ever attempted such a subject.

Her aunt suddenly seemed to sense Zoe's scrutiny, and turned, her face hard and oddly set.

'So here you are.' Her greeting was abrupt. 'You're very late.'

'There was a staff meeting,' Zoe returned with equal brevity. 'You should have let me know you were coming, Aunt Megan.' She paused. 'Would you like some tea?'

'No, this isn't a social call.' The older woman seated herself in the high-backed armchair beside the empty fire-place.

My mother's chair, Zoe thought with a pang, trying not to feel resentful. It was, after all, her aunt's house, but it was small wonder there'd been friction in the past if she made a habit of walking in whenever the whim took her.

Megan Arnold was dressed as usual in a pleated navy skirt with a matching hand-knitted jacket over a tailored pale blue blouse, and her greying hair was drawn back from her thin face in a severe knot.

'As you can see I've placed the house on the market,' she went on. 'I've instructed the agents to commence show-ing the property at once, so you'll have to remove all this clutter.' She waved a hand at the books and ornaments that filled the shelves on either side of the fireplace. Then paused. 'I'd be obliged if you'd remove yourself, too, by the end of the month.'

Zoe gasped helplessly. 'Just like that?'

'What did you expect?' Megan Arnold's mouth was a hard line. 'My husband allowed your mother to have this property for *her* lifetime only. The arrangement did not mention you. You surely weren't expecting to stay on here,' she added sharply.

'I wasn't expecting anything,' Zoe said, with equal crisp-ness. 'But I did think I'd be allowed some kind of breathing space.'

'I feel you've had plenty of time.' The other woman was unmoved. 'And in the eyes of the law, you're merely squat-ting here.' She paused. 'You should have no difficulty in finding a bedsitting room in Bishops Cross itself. Some-where convenient for your work.'

'A bedsit would hardly be adequate,' Zoe said, keeping tight hold on her control. George must have known about this, she thought with shock. His mother must have told him what her aunt was planning. Or he heard them talking one day at the house. And that's why he asked me to marry him. Because he knew I was going to be virtually homeless almost at once.

She shivered. Oh, George, why didn't you warn me in-stead of trying to play Sir Galahad? she thought desper-ately.

She drew a deep, steadying breath. Did her best to speak normally. 'Not all the furniture came with the cottage. Some of it belonged to Mother, and I'll want to take it with me, as well as her books and pictures.'

She saw Megan Arnold's gaze go back to the painting above the mantelpiece, and decided, however belatedly, to try an overture. To heal a breach that had never been of her making. 'Maybe you'd like to have one of them your-self, as a keepsake,' she suggested. 'That one, perhaps.'

Her aunt almost recoiled. 'Wretched daub.' Her voice shook. 'I wouldn't have it in the house.'

Zoe stared at her, appalled at the anger, the bitterness in her tone. She said slowly, 'Aunt Megan—why—why do you hate her so much?'

'What are you talking about? I—hate Gina—the perfect sister?' Her sudden laugh was shrill. 'What nonsense. No one was allowed to hate her. Not ever. Whatever she did, however great the sin, she was loved and forgiven always. By everyone.'

'She's dead, Aunt Megan.' Against her will, Zoe's voice broke. 'If she ever hurt you, I'm sure it wasn't intentional. And, anyway, she can't do so again.'

'You're wrong.' Mrs Arnold lifted her chin coldly. 'She never had the power to affect me in any way. Because I always saw her for what she was. That innocent, butter-wouldn't-melt façade never fooled me for a minute. And how right I was.'

She stopped abruptly. 'But that's all in the past, and the future is what matters. Selling this cottage for a start.' She stood up. 'I suggest you hire a skip for all this rubbish—or take it to a car-boot sale. Whatever you decide, I want it cleared before the first viewers arrive. Starting with this.'

She reached up and lugged the Mediterranean painting off its hook, tossing it contemptuously down onto the rug in front of the hearth. There was an ominous cracking sound.

'The frame,' Zoe whispered. She went down on one knee, almost protectively. 'You've broken it.' She looked up, shaking her head. 'How could you?'

Her aunt shrugged, a touch defensively. 'It was loose anyway. Cheap wood, and poorly made.'

'Whatever.' Zoe was almost choking. 'You had no right—no right to *touch* it.'

'This is my property. I shall do what I wish.' Her aunt reached for her bag. 'And I want the rest removed, and all the holes in the plaster made good,' she added. 'I shall be back at the end of the week to make sure my instructions are being followed. Or I shall arrange a house clearance myself.'

She swept out, and a moment later Zoe, still kneeling on the rug, heard the front door slam.

To be followed almost immediately by the back door opening, and Adele calling to her.

'Jeff's looking after the kids,' she announced as she came in. 'I saw Madam leaving, and came to make sure you're all right.'

Zoe shook her head. 'I feel as if I've been hit by a train,' she admitted. She swallowed. 'God, she was vile. I—I can't believe it.'

'I'll put the kettle on,' said Adele. She paused. 'What happened to the picture?'

'She threw it on the floor. It was completely crazy. I

mean, I don't think it's necessarily the best thing my mother ever did, and it spent most of its life up in the attic until she moved here, but…' She paused, lost for words.

'Well, I've always liked it,' Adele said. 'Greece, isn't it? My sister gets concessionary rates, so we went to Crete last year, and Corfu the year before.'

Zoe shrugged. 'It's somewhere in that region, I guess.' She gave it a doubtful look, then got to her feet, holding the damaged frame carefully, and placed the picture on the sofa. 'Only we've never been there. My father didn't like very hot weather.'

'Well, perhaps she copied a postcard or something that someone sent her,' Adele suggested as she filled the kettle in the kitchen.

'Maybe.' Zoe frowned. 'It was one of those things I always meant to ask about, but never did.'

'So, when are you being evicted?' Adele asked as they sat at the kitchen table, drinking their tea.

'I have to be out by the end of the month,' Zoe admitted. 'And she means it.'

'Hmm.' Adele was thoughtful for a moment. 'Do you think she really is crazy?'

'Not certifiably,' Zoe said wryly. 'Just totally irrational where my mother is concerned.'

'Well, maybe that's not entirely her fault,' Adele said meditatively. 'My gran remembers her as a child, and she said she was a nice-looking kid, and the apple of her parents' eye. Then your sister came along, as an afterthought, and immediately she was the favourite. And "the pretty one", too.'

She shrugged. 'That can't have been very nice. And not easy for any kid to handle. So, maybe it's just common or garden jealousy.'

'From Queen of the Castle to the Queen in *Snow White*?' Zoe pondered. 'Well, you could be right, but I have the feeling there's more to it than that.'

'And it won't help that you're the image of your mum

at the same age.' Adele poured more tea into her mug.
'Though they weren't always bad friends—according to
Gran, anyway,' she added thoughtfully. 'There was a time
when they did things together—even went away on holiday. Although even then your aunt behaved more as if she
was her mother than her sister by all accounts.' She pursed
her lips. 'Maybe that's what caused the trouble.'

She paused. 'So what are you going to do? How are you
going to manage, if she's turning you out?'

Zoe grimaced. 'I'm going to have to find a flat—unfur-
nished.'

'Or even a small house. You'll miss the garden.'

'Yes.' Zoe's lip quivered suddenly. 'Among so many
other things.' She forced herself to smile. 'Maybe Aunt
Megan's doing me a favour. I'd just been thinking that my
life could do with a whole new direction. This could be
exactly the impetus I need. I might even move right away
from here.'

'Some place where the wicked Queen can't barge in,
using her own key,' Adele agreed. 'Although I'd miss you.'

'Well, I won't be going immediately.' Zoe wrinkled her
nose. 'My contract stipulates one full term's notice. But I
can be looking—and planning.'

'You don't think some prince on a white horse is going
to gallop up and rescue you?' Adele asked, deadpan.

One already tried, thought Zoe, but he drives a Metro,
and always stays inside the speed limit. And, anyway, I'm
not sure who'd be rescuing whom…

'Not in Bishops Cross,' she returned, also straight-faced.
'White horses can't cope with the one-way traffic system.'

She finished her tea, and put the mug in the sink. 'I'd
better arrange to have my mother's things taken out and
stored in the short term,' she mused aloud. 'Aunt Megan
mentioned a skip,' she added with a touch of grimness.
'And I'd put nothing past her.'

'Not after that picture,' said Adele. 'Pity about that. Nice
and bright, I always thought.'

'It's not terminally damaged—just needs a new frame. I'll take it in with me tomorrow.'

'It'll be awkward on the bus. And there's a framing shop a couple of doors from where Jeff works. Why don't I ask him to drop it off for you on his way to work? Then you can pop round in your lunch break and choose another frame. Just tie a bit of paper and string round it, and I'll take it with me now.'

'Oh, Adele, that would be kind.'

Adele had always been a good neighbour, Zoe reflected as she hunted for the string. And, after Aunt Megan, her cheerful practicality was balm to the spirit.

'She's made a real mess of it,' Adele commented grimly as Zoe went back into the sitting room. 'Even the backing's torn away.' She tried to smooth it back into place, and paused. 'Just a minute. There's something down inside it. Look.' She delved into the back of the picture, and came up with a bulky and clearly elderly manilla envelope.

She handed it to Zoe who stood, weighing it in her hands, staring down at it with an odd feeling of unease.

'Well, aren't you going to open it?' Adele prompted after a moment. She laughed. 'If it was me, I couldn't wait.'

'Yes,' Zoe said, slowly. 'I—I suppose so. But the fact is, it has been waiting—for a pretty long time, by the look of it. And, as my mother must have put it there, I'm wondering why she didn't tell me about it—if she wanted me to find it, that is.'

Adele shrugged. 'I expect she forgot about it.'

'How could she? It's been hanging there over the mantelpiece ever since she moved here—a constant reminder.' Zoe shook her head. 'It's something she wanted to keep secret, Adele, when I didn't think we had any secrets between us.' She tried to smile. 'And that's come as a bit of a shock.'

Adele patted her on the shoulder. 'It's been quite a day for them. Why don't I leave you in peace while you decide what to do? You can bring the picture round later on, if you still want it re-framing.'

Left to herself, Zoe sank down on the sofa. There was no message on the envelope, she realised. No 'For my daughter' or 'To be opened in the event of my death'.

This was something that had remained hidden and private in Gina Lambert's life. And if Aunt Megan hadn't totally lost it, and thrown the picture on the floor, it would probably have stayed that way.

Maybe that was how it should be left. Maybe she should respect her mother's tacit wish, and put it in the bin unopened.

Yet if I do that, Zoe thought, I shall always wonder…

With sudden resolution, she tore open the envelope and extracted the contents. There was quite an assortment, ranging from a bulky legal-looking document to some photographs.

She unfolded the document first, her brows snapping together as she realised it was written in a foreign language. Greek, she thought in bewilderment as she studied the unfamiliar alphabet. It's in Greek, of all things. Why on earth would Mother have such a thing?

She put it down, and began to examine the photographs. Most of them seemed to be local scenes—a village street lined with white houses—a market, its stalls groaning with fruit—an old woman in black, leading a donkey laden with firewood.

One, however, was completely different. A garden guarded by tall cypresses, and a man, casually dressed in shorts and a shirt, standing beneath one of the trees. His face was in shadow, but some instinct told her that he was not English, and that he was looking back at whoever was holding the camera, and smiling.

And she knew, without question, that he was smiling at her mother.

She turned her head and studied the framed photograph of her father that occupied pride of place on the side table beside her mother's chair. But she knew already that the shadow man was not John Lambert. The shape was all wrong, she thought. He'd been taller, for one thing, and thinner, and the man in the snapshot seemed, in some strange way and even at this distance in time and place, to exude a kind of raw energy that her father had not possessed.

Zoe swallowed. I don't understand any of this, she thought. And I'm not sure I want to.

She felt very much as if she'd opened Pandora's box, and was not convinced that Hope would be waiting for her at the end.

She turned the snapshot over, hoping to find some clue— a name, perhaps, scribbled on the back. But there was nothing. Slowly and carefully, she put it aside with the rest, and turned to the other papers.

There were several thin sheets stapled together, and when she unfolded them she realised, with sudden excitement, that this must be a translation of the Greek legal document that had so puzzled her.

She read them through eagerly, then paused, and went back to the beginning again, her brain whirling. Because the stilted, formal language was telling her that this was a deed of gift, assigning to her mother the Villa Danae, near a place called Livassi, on the island of Thania.

Zoe felt stunned, not merely by the discovery, but by its implications.

This was a gift that Gina Lambert had never mentioned, and certainly never used. And that she'd clearly not wanted known. That she'd hidden in the back of a picture, which itself suddenly assumed a whole new significance.

Was it the recapturing of a cherished, but secret memory? Certainly that was how it seemed, particularly when she recalled how it had never been on show during John Lambert's lifetime.

She read the translation through a third time. The name of the gift's donor was not mentioned, she noticed, although she guessed it would be in the original. And there were no restrictions on the villa's ownership either. It was Gina's to pass on to her heirs, or sell, as she wished.

Yet there was nothing in the few remaining papers, consisting of a few tourist leaflets, a bill from a Hotel Stavros, and a ferry ticket, to indicate that she'd disposed of the Villa Danae.

And she left me everything, thought Zoe, swallowing. So, unlikely as it seems, I now own a villa in Greece.

She realised she was shaking uncontrollably, her heart thudding like a trip-hammer. She made herself stand and walk over to the cupboard where her mother's precious bottle of Napoleon brandy still resided, and poured herself a generous measure. Emergency tactics, she told herself.

When she was calmer, she fetched the atlas, and looked to see where Thania was. It was a small island in the Ionian sea, and Livassi seemed to be its capital, and only large town.

Not very revealing, Zoe thought, wrinkling her nose.

But Adele's sister works in a travel agency, she reminded herself. She'd be able to tell me all about it—and how to get there.

Because she had to go to Thania, there was no question about that. She had to see the Villa Danae for herself—if it was still standing. After all, it had belonged to an absentee owner for a long time, and might be in a state of real neglect and disrepair. But I have to know, she thought, taking another swift swig of her brandy as her pulses began to gallop again. And I have some money saved, and the whole summer vacation in front of me. There'll never be a better opportunity.

She wouldn't keep the house, of course. If it was habitable, she'd put it on the market. If it was falling down, she would just have to walk away—as her mother, apparently, had done before her.

But I'm not just going to see the villa, she thought. I want to find the answers to some questions as well. I need the truth, however painful, before I move on—start my new life.

She picked up the photo of the shadow man, and stood, staring down at him, wondering, and a little scared at the same time. Asking herself who he could be, and what his part in this mystery might be.

She sighed abruptly, and hid him back in the envelope with the rest of the paperwork.

I'll find you, too, she thought. Somewhere. Somehow. And whatever the cost.

And tried to ignore the involuntary little shiver of misgiving that tingled down her spine.

CHAPTER TWO

THE rail of the boat was hot under Zoe's bare arm. Ahead of her, the craggy outline of Thania rose from the shimmer of the sea.

Even now, with her target in sight, Zoe could still hardly believe she was doing this. The tension inside her was like a knot, endlessly being pulled more tightly.

She had told no one the real purpose of her visit to the island, not even Adele. She'd pretended that the envelope had merely contained souvenirs of what had been, clearly, a holiday her mother had once enjoyed, but memorable to no one but herself, and consequently not worth mentioning.

'I need a break, so why don't I try and discover what she found so entrancing?' she'd laughed.

'Well, don't be too entranced,' Adele warned. 'And don't let any local Adonis chat you on board his boat,' she added severely. 'We don't want you doing a Shirley Valentine. You have to come back.'

I'm my mother's daughter, Zoe thought wryly. And she came back, whatever the incentive to stay.

Aloud, she said lightly, 'No danger.'

She'd told the same story of her mother's favourite island to Adele's sister Vanessa when she made the booking at the travel agency. Notwithstanding, Vanessa had tried hard to talk her into going somewhere larger and livelier.

'Thania's never been a typical tourist resort,' she'd protested. 'A number of rich Athenians have homes there, and they like to keep the hordes at bay. The hotels are small, and the beaches are mostly private. It's all low-key and the nightlife barely exists. The ferry runs just twice a day from Kefalonia.'

She brightened. 'Why don't you stay on Kefalonia instead? See all the places where they filmed *Captain Corelli's Mandolin*. There's plenty to do there, and you could always go on a day trip to Thania if you really want to see it.'

Zoe shook her head, keeping her face solemn. 'Nicholas Cage went back to America a long time ago, so I think I'll pass on Kefalonia this time around. Besides, somewhere small and peaceful is exactly what I want.' She paused, then tried to sound casual. 'I believe there's a Hotel Stavros in Livassi. Maybe you could book me in there.'

Vanessa stabbed frowningly at her computer keys, then nodded with a touch of resignation. 'Argonaut Holidays go there, one of the few companies that do, and they have vacancies, surprise, surprise.' She stabbed again. 'Bath, balcony, sea view?'

Terrace, thought Zoe, with steps leading up to it, and the sea beyond...

She smiled. 'Ideal.'

She'd met with downright disapproval from George, who was still plainly disappointed that she'd gently but firmly turned down his proposal. 'But you never go abroad on holiday.' He sounded injured.

'No, George,' she said, still gently but firmly. 'I never have in the past, that's all.'

'But if you'd mentioned it sooner, we could have gone somewhere together,' he protested. 'My mother did a tour a couple of years back—"The Treasures of Italy". She enjoyed it, and the hotels were of a high standard. We could have done the same thing.' He paused awkwardly. 'I understand Greek plumbing is—rather eccentric.'

'I know,' she said. 'They told me all about it at the travel agency, and it's not a problem.' She gave him a steady look. 'Besides, George, your mother would never have let you go on holiday with me—even if we'd been married.'

He flushed uncomfortably. 'You're wrong, Zoe. She's

always telling people how happy she'd be to have me off her hands—to have grandchildren.'

Certainly, thought Zoe, if it could be done by divine intervention, without having an all too human daughter-in-law in the equation.

'So where exactly are you going?' he asked.

Zoe shrugged, trying not to look shifty. 'I thought I'd do some island hopping—never too long in one place. See what appeals,' she told him airily.

She hated fibbing to George, but she knew his mother would have her destination out of him before his supper was on the table, and Aunt Megan would be next in line for the information. And, given her aunt's extreme reaction to the picture, this would be bad news.

What a pity, she thought, that I can't go to her. Ask her about it. Because she must know. I'm sure of that.

She hadn't seen Mrs Arnold since that day, not even when she'd taken the cottage keys round to the house and dropped them through the letterbox. Her aunt had probably been at home, but there had seemed little point in another confrontation, whatever its purpose.

And she'd been frantically busy. In addition to the usual end of term workload, she'd managed to find herself temporary accommodation in a top-floor flat in an old Victorian house within walking distance of the college. It was furnished and the rent was reasonable, enabling her to put her mother's cherished pieces in store for the future.

Which was something else she hadn't mentioned to George—the fact that she'd given in her notice at the college and would be leaving at Christmas. Finding another job in a different area. A challenge that awaited her when she got back from Greece.

'Ah, well, "sufficient unto the day",' she told herself silently.

She took a bottle of water from her shoulder bag, and drank thirstily. As she replaced the bottle she heard the crackle of paper, reminding her of the purpose of her visit.

She'd brought the Greek deed of gift, together with the translation, and the photographs. But she had no intention of barging in and making a claim straight away.

First, she told herself, I need to find out how the land lies. For all I know, the villa's original owner may have had second thoughts and revoked the gift years ago.

So I'll find the house, and see who's living there now. And if it's obvious that giving it away was just a temporary aberration on someone's part a long time ago, then I'll just enjoy my holiday, and no harm done.

After all, it is a little bit too much like a fairy tale.

The Villa Danae, she thought. She'd checked in a book of Greek myths and discovered that Danae had been one of the many loved by Zeus, who had visited her in a stream of golden light. She'd subsequently given birth to Perseus and been set adrift on the ocean with her baby in a locked chest, but they'd both survived and Perseus had gone on to cut off the head of the Gorgon Medusa, and win the hand of Andromeda.

This is my own quest, she thought. My private odyssey. And decapitation will probably not be involved.

The harbour at Thania was only small, and occupied mainly by caiques rather than expensive yachts. The town itself was built on the side of a steep hill, with serried ranks of red-roofed houses looking as if they might tumble forward into the sea. On the quayside ahead, Zoe could see the striped awnings of tavernas, and among them a larger building, three storeys high, its white paint gleaming in the sunlight, which she knew from the picture in the Argonaut brochure was the Hotel Stavros.

It was mid-afternoon, by this time, and the heat was intense. Zoe had dressed for coolness in white cut-off trousers, and a sleeveless navy top, knotted at the midriff. She'd covered her exposed skin in high-factor sunblock, and braided her hair into one thick plait, cramming over it a wide-brimmed linen hat.

Ready for anything, she thought, briskly swinging up her travel bag as the ferry moved into its allotted place on the dock. There were few other passengers, and those, she guessed, were locals rather than tourists.

Zoe was aware she was being surveyed with friendly interest, and as she went ashore, treading gingerly down the rickety gangplank, the captain gave her a gap-toothed smile and a hoarse grunt of appreciation.

No point trying to hide herself in the crowd, then, she decided, amused.

She made straight for the hotel, climbing two steps to the terrace with its tables and chairs, and tubs planted cheerfully with pelargoniums. Inside the double glass doors, the tiled reception area was apparently deserted, but Zoe was glad to stand and catch her breath for a moment, in its air-conditioned coolness.

And, as if on cue, the fringed curtain at the rear of the desk stirred, and a girl, plump, red-haired and smiling, emerged to meet her.

'Hi,' she greeted Zoe casually. 'You must be Miss Lambert. I'm Sherry.'

'And you're British.' Zoe shook hands with her, smiling back. 'I didn't expect that.'

'And I didn't expect to meet and marry a Greek hotel owner two years ago,' the other girl admitted candidly. 'So, it's a bit of a novelty for me, too.' She handed Zoe a registration card and a pen.

'I'll show you your room,' she went on, taking down a key from a rack on the wall behind her. 'Leave your bag, and Stavros will bring it up in a minute.'

'The Stavros for whom the hotel was named?' Zoe asked, trying to do mental sums about his possible age.

Sherry shook her head, leading the way up a marble staircase. 'That was his uncle—a real character. Great eye for the ladies even now. Never married because he thought it would cramp his style,' she added with a rich chuckle. 'My Stavros took over the hotel when he decided to retire a few

years ago. Now he sits under the trees in the square, playing
lethal games of backgammon.'

'Sounds a marvellous life,' Zoe said, committing all this
information to memory.

'Here we are.' Sherry threw open a door, allowing Zoe
to precede her into a cool, shadowy room, its shutters
closed against the glare of the sun. Sherry pulled back the
thin drapes and unlatched the shutters, revealing spotless
cream walls to match the tiled floor. There was a cupboard
built into one wall with a hanging rail, and a modest chest
of drawers beside the low bed, with its crisp, snowy linen,
and terracotta coverlet folded back across the foot.

'It's lovely,' Zoe said with total sincerity.

'If you need a blanket, which I doubt, just ask.' Sherry
opened another door. 'And this is your shower room. It's
pretty basic—you sit on that little wooden bench to wash,
and all the water goes down that drain in the middle, as
you see—but you can generally have a warm shower when
you want one.' She paused. 'I'll leave you to look round.
Can I get you a drink—a cold beer, maybe—or some lemon
tea?'

'Tea would be wonderful,' Zoe accepted gratefully. Left
to herself, she stepped out onto the balcony, finding to her
pleasure that her room overlooked the harbour.

She could quite see why her mother had loved it here,
no matter what might or might not have befallen her.

A tap on the door, signalling the arrival of her luggage,
brought her back into the room.

Stavros was dark and swarthy, with a quiet, courteous
manner. 'My wife wishes to know if you would like your
tea in your room, *kyria*, or downstairs in our courtyard?'

'Oh, downstairs, I think. I only need a few minutes to
unpack.'

The courtyard was at the rear of the hotel, shaded by a
massive vine. Zoe sat at a corner, sipping her tea and considering her immediate options. At some point she would
have to seek out Uncle Stavros of the roving eye, she

thought, and see if, by some remote chance, he remembered
her mother. Any information she could glean would be wel
come, she acknowledged with a faint sigh.

A large hairy dog, resembling a moving hearthrug, came
sauntering out of the hotel and ambled up to her, panting
amiably, and clearly waiting to have his head scratched and
his floppy ears gently pulled.

'You're a good boy,' Zoe told him softly as she com
plied. She would have a dog, she thought, when she found
a place of her own to live. Her mother had wanted one a
the cottage, but Aunt Megan had instantly vetoed the idea

'Don't let Archimedes be a nuisance,' Sherry warned
when she came to collect the tray.

'Why on earth did you call him that?' Zoe asked, in
trigued.

'Because he once climbed in the bath with Stavros and
nearly flooded the place.' Sherry stroked the untidy head
'He's now barred for life from all bathrooms.'

'While we're on the subject of water,' Zoe said, laugh
ing, 'where's the best place to swim from?'

Sherry considered. 'There's the town beach,' she said
'Turn left out of the hotel, and keep walking. It's not bad
but it can get pretty crowded. There are some good beache
on the other side of the island, but you can only reach then
by boat, and Stavros sometimes gets up a trip for guests i
enough are interested.

'Apart from that…' She pulled a face, and took a swif
look round. 'Not all the villa owners are here the whol
time, and we occasionally take advantage of that, and use
their beaches when they're away. What the eye don't see,
she added cheerfully. 'But don't tell Stavros I said so, be
cause he gets twitchy.'

She lowered her voice confidentially. 'As a matter o
fact, one villa overlooks a really pretty cove, but it's no
used because the place has never been lived in. I go down
there sometimes, although Stavros isn't very happy abou

it. He has a real thing about privacy, and upsetting the owners.'

Zoe swallowed. 'But if it's not used, it sounds ideal,' she said huskily. 'Maybe you could give me directions.' She paused. 'Does it have a name—this house?'

'Mmm.' Sherry nodded as she prepared to depart. 'The Villa Danae. You could walk there,' she added over her shoulder.

I not only could, Zoe thought exultantly, when she was alone. I will. Tomorrow.

Half-buried in long grass, the small wooden board was shaped like an arrow and pointed down a narrow dusty track. The faded words 'Villa Danae' were only just legible, as Sherry had quietly warned her as Zoe had eaten her breakfast of warm rolls, flower-scented honey, and thick, creamy yoghurt.

Now she paused, hitching the cream canvas bag that held her towel, sun lotion and paperback novel into a more comfortable position on her shoulder.

Even though she'd been waiting for this moment, she was sorely tempted to walk on. To let the past rest in peace. To go with the flow, and let herself be absorbed effortlessly into Thania's languorous charm. To simply have a much-needed vacation.

But that would not quell the wondering, she told herself. And when she got back, and saw Gina's picture newly framed and hanging in her bedroom, she might kick herself for wasting a golden opportunity.

She turned with renewed determination, and plunged down the rutted track. It led down through a grove of olive trees, and, although it was still comparatively early in the day, she was grateful for their silvery shade. The air was very still, and the cloudless sky had a faintly misty look that promised soaring temperatures to come.

She was wearing a thin, floating sundress, sleeveless and

scoop-necked, in gentian-blue, over a matching bikini, and her hair was piled up in a loose knot on top of her head.

She rounded a steep bend in the track, and saw, beyond the shelter of the olive grove, the more vivid green of grass and colourful splashes of flowers. Not the desolate wilderness she'd half expected. And a little further on, set like a jewel in the encircling garden, was the house, all immaculate white walls and terracotta roof.

Zoe paused, her hand tightening unconsciously round the strap of her bag. Immediately in front of her was the turquoise gleam of a swimming pool, from which a flight of broad, shallow steps led up to sliding glass doors. Behind these was a low, pillared room like an atrium, cool with marble and towering green plants, and furnished with comfortable white chairs and loungers.

Trying not to feel too much like an intruder, Zoe skirted the pool, climbed the steps and tried the doors, but they were securely locked.

It's like looking into a showcase, she thought as she walked on. You can admire, but not touch.

And halted abruptly, her heart jolting as she reached the foot of another flight of steps, so immediately familiar she could have climbed them in her sleep. Pale steps, she recognised breathlessly, dusty with the faded blossoms of the bougainvillea that cascaded down the side of the house. Steps that led up to a terrace, its balustrade supporting a large stone urn, heavy with clustering flowers. As she'd known there would be. And beyond that the dreamy azure of the sea.

She steadied herself, then, quietly and cautiously, she climbed up to the terrace. She found herself standing on a broad sweep of creamy marble that ran the entire length of the house. Stone troughs massed with more flowers marked the length of the waist-high balustrade, while below it, from a gated opening, another curved flight of steps led down through cypress trees standing like sentries to a perfect horseshoe of pale sand, and the vivid blue ripple of the sea.

Behind her, shuttered glass doors masked the ground floor rooms completely. But what had she expected? The place laid open for her inspection, and a welcome mat waiting?

I should have gone to see a lawyer, she told herself restively, walking along the terrace. Had the whole legal situation checked out. Approaches made.

She found the main entrance round the corner, a solid wooden door, heavily carved, and growing beside it, in festoons of blooms that softened the dark wood and white walls, an exquisite climbing rose, its petals shading from creamy yellow to deep gold.

Zoe found herself thinking of the shower of radiance in which Zeus had come to Danae in the legend, then told herself she was being fanciful. Whoever had planted the garden had simply loved roses, that was all. The troughs and urns along the terrace had been fragrant with them, and she could see even more in the beds that bordered the lawn. And sexual predators in Greek mythology had nothing to do with it.

Without knowing why, she stretched out a hand and touched one of the heavy golden heads, almost as if it were a lucky charm. Then she reached for the heavy iron door handle and tried it.

To her amazement, it yielded, and the door opened silently on well-oiled hinges. The Villa Danae was welcoming her, after all.

She stepped inside and closed the door behind her, standing for a moment, listening intently for a footfall, a door closing, a cough. The sound of a human presence to explain the unlocked door. But there was nothing.

She found herself in a wide hall, confronted by a sweep of staircase leading up to a galleried landing. On one side of it was the glass wall of the atrium. On the other were more conventional doors leading to a long living room, where chairs and sofas were grouped round an empty fireplace. A deep alcove at the far end of the room contained a dining table and chairs.

Everything was in pristine condition. No one had ever lounged on those cushions, she thought, or lit a fire in that hearth, or eaten a meal at the table.

On the atrium side, she found a tiled and fully fitted kitchen, with a walk-in food store, and a laundry room leading off it, all of them bare as if they'd been somehow frozen in time, and were waiting for the spell to be broken.

Taking a deep breath, Zoe went upstairs, annoyed to find she was tiptoeing.

The first room she came to was the master bedroom, dim and cool behind its shutters. She trod across the floor, unlatched the heavy wooden slats and pulled them open, then turned, catching her breath.

It was a vast and luxurious room, with apricot walls and an ivory tiled floor. The silk bed covering was ivory, too, as were the voile drapes that hung at the windows.

There was a bathroom with a screened-off shower cubicle, and a sunken bath with taps like smiling dolphins, and a dressing room as well. There were toiletries on the tiled surfaces, and fluffy towels on the rails. Everything in its place—an enchanted palace waiting for its princess. But for how long?

Zoe walked slowly back to the window, and slid it open with care, then stepped out onto the balcony, lifting her face to the slight breeze. Before her were the misty shapes of other islands rising out of the unruffled blue of the Ionian sea.

More roses here, too, she saw, spilling over the balcony rail from their pottery tubs in a cascade of cream and gold. Their scent reached her softly, and she breathed it in, feeling herself become part of the enchantment.

She thought, Can this really be mine?

And in the same heartbeat, realised she was not alone after all. That there was someone below her on the terrace.

She froze, then peered with infinite caution over the balcony rail.

A man, she registered, with his back to her, moving unhurriedly along the terrace, removing the dead heads from the blossoms in the stone troughs.

The gardener, she thought with relief. Only the gardener. One of the support team employed to keep Villa Danae in this immaculate condition.

He was tall, with a mane of curling black hair that gleamed like silk in the sunlight, his skin like burnished bronze against the brief pair of elderly white shorts that were all he was wearing. She saw broad shoulders, and a muscular back, narrowing to lean hips, and long, sinewy legs.

The kind of Adonis, she thought, with a faint catch of the breath, that Adele had warned her about.

Of course, she could only see his back view, so he might well have a squint, a crooked nose, and dribble. But somehow she didn't think so.

And anyway, his looks were not her concern. What she needed to do was get out of here before he looked up and saw her.

With infinite caution, she backed away into the room. She dragged at the windows, tugging them together. They came with a whisper, but, to Zoe's overwrought imagination, it seemed like a rumble of thunder in the stillness of the morning. She waited for a shout from below. The sound of an alarm being given, but there was nothing, and, biting her lip, she closed the shutters, too. So far, so good, she thought with a tiny sigh of relief.

His work seemed to be taking him to the far end of the terrace, away from the main door, so if she was quick she could be out of the villa and back into the shelter of the olive grove before she ran any real risk of discovery.

And she would content herself with just this one visit, she promised herself silently as she let herself out of the bedroom and closed the door quietly behind her. After all, she had seen everything she needed to see.

From now on she would stick firmly to the town beach, and let her lawyer investigate whether or not the Villa Danae was her inheritance.

Well, she thought, smiling. I can dream, I suppose.

She had taken three steps down the stairs before she realised she was not alone. And just who was standing at the bottom of the flight, leaning casually on the polished rail, watching her—waiting for her, a faint grim smile playing round his mouth.

She checked with a gasp, turned to stone at the sight of him. Her instinct was to turn and run back the way she'd come, but common sense prevented her. This staircase was the only way out, and the last thing she wanted was to find herself trapped in a bedroom with this half-naked stranger in pursuit.

She was frightened, but at the same time—incredibly—her senses were registering other things. Telling her that the man confronting her with such cool arrogance was as seriously attractive as her instinct had suggested. Not conventionally handsome, maybe. His high-bridged nose was too thin, and his mouth and chin too hard for that. And his eyes were darkness. Meeting his gaze was like staring into impenetrable night, she thought, tension tautening her throat.

But, at the same time, she knew instinctively that there wasn't a woman in the world who would take one glance and not want to look again—and again. Because he was totally and compellingly male.

He said quietly, *'Kalimera.'*

Maybe, she thought breathlessly. Maybe there was a way she could bluff her way out of this.

She spread her hands. Tried an apologetic laugh. 'I'm sorry—I don't understand. I don't speak Greek.'

He shrugged. 'Then we will speak in English. It's not a

problem,' he added drily as her face fell. 'Tell me what you are doing here.'

She said swiftly, 'I'm not a thief.'

'No,' he agreed thoughtfully. 'Because there is nothing here that you could conveniently steal.' The dark glance swept her, assessing the flimsy blue dress, the canvas beach bag. 'Or hide,' he added.

He looked her over again, more searchingly. 'So, I ask again—what is your reason for being here?'

'Someone mentioned there was a house for sale round here,' Zoe improvised swiftly. 'I thought it might be this one, as it's obviously empty.'

'No,' he said. 'It is not this house.' He paused, his gaze steady and ironic. 'And no one would have told you that it was.' His voice was low-pitched but crisp.

'You don't think the owner might have put it on the market and not told you?' she parried.

'No,' he said. 'That would not happen either.'

'Well, it's still a fabulous house.' Zoe lifted her chin. 'Maybe the owner would be prepared to rent it out.'

His brows rose. 'You have nowhere to stay?'

'Yes,' she said. 'Of course I have. But this is such a lovely island. Perhaps I could come back—stay longer.'

'You arrived—when?' His mouth twisted. 'Yesterday?'

'It doesn't take long,' she said. 'To find something— beautiful. And decide you want more.'

The dark eyes looked her up and down again with mockery in their depths—and something infinitely more disturbing. 'Well, we agree on something at least,' he drawled, and laughed as the sudden colour drenched her skin.

She was suddenly stingingly aware of all that tanned bare skin, so negligently displayed, and also how little she herself was wearing. And how this had not escaped him for a minute.

She wished with all her heart that she were sitting at her table under the vine leaves, finishing breakfast, and contemplating nothing more risky than a day on the town beach.

Because she was in danger. Every nerve in her body was telling her so.

Just let me get out of here, relatively unscathed, she prayed silently and wildly.

'Now let me tell you how I see the situation,' he went on, almost casually. 'I think you are staying at the Hotel Stavros. That Stavros' wife has told you the cove that belongs to the house is good to bathe from, and that she comes here herself—not often but enough, and thinks that no one knows. And that once here, because you are a woman, you could not control your curiosity. So, you found an open door, and came in.'

She hated herself for blushing. Hated him more for having made her do it. She said coldly, 'You're right, up to a point. But I was intrigued to hear the house was empty, because I might actually be interested in—acquiring it.'

'And I have told you,' he said. 'It is not for sale.'

'Really?' She shrugged a shoulder. 'Well, that's not something I choose to discuss with the hired help.' She paused to allow that to sink in, and was annoyed to see his smile widen. 'Is the owner on Thania at present?'

'No,' he said. 'Athens.'

She wanted to say, That's what you think, and wave the deed of gift in his face, yet caution prevailed.

But, there will come a time, she promised herself. And anticipation will make it all the sweeter. Because the first Greek phrase I shall learn is 'You're fired'.

She allowed herself a slight frown. Regaining lost ground, she told herself. Deliberately establishing a formal distance between them. Someone with business to transact dealing with a minor member of staff. That was how to handle things.

'That's a pity,' she said. 'But I suppose there's someone on the island who can tell me how I could contact him.'

'Why, yes, *thespinis*. You could always ask me.' His face was solemn, but his voice quivered with amusement, leaving her with the uneasy feeling that he knew exactly what she was doing.

She lifted her chin. 'I hardly think I should approach him through his gardener,' she said sharply.

'But I am not merely the gardener,' he said, softly. 'I take care of a great many things for him. But if you wish to speak to him directly, he will soon be here on Thania. Within a week, I believe.'

'And staying here?'

'No,' he said, after a pause. 'He never stays here. He has a villa of his own quite near.'

'That's such a shame,' Zoe said, and meant it. 'It's a wonderful house, but it's bound to deteriorate if it isn't lived in—and loved.'

'You are wrong, *thespinis*,' he said. 'One thing this house has never lacked is love. It was built into every wall—every beam—every stone. Love is the reason it exists.'

She was shaken by the sudden passion in his voice—and by the odd raw note of anger, too.

She said, with a touch of uncertainty, 'I'll wait, then—and speak to him. When he arrives.' She paused. 'And now I'd better go.'

'And where will you go?' That strange, harsh moment had passed and he was smiling again, the dark eyes speculative as they studied her. 'Down to the cove as you intended?'

Zoe bit her lip. 'No—that was a bad idea, and I'm sorry.'

'Why?' he said. 'The sea is warm, and the sand inviting. And you will not be disturbed.'

She was already disturbed, she thought. Stirred in every fibre of her being, and it was not a sensation she relished, or even wished to admit.

Turned on by a good-looking Greek, she derided herself. How shameful—and how pathetic.

She shrugged, attempted a smile of her own. 'All the same…'

'You like his house,' he said. 'I am sure my employer would wish you also to enjoy his beach. There is a way down from the terrace. I will show you.'

'I really don't think…'

'Is that why you came to Thania—to think?' He straightened in a leisurely manner, moving back a little. Offering her, she realised, free passage past him. 'Then stop thinking, *thespinis*. Learn to relax. Begin—to feel.'

'Perhaps, then,' she said. Adding primly, 'But I don't want to take you away from your work.'

'You will not,' he said. 'But my work, alas, will take me away from you. So, you see,' he added gently, 'there is nothing to fear.'

Zoe stiffened. 'I'm not in the least afraid,' she told him curtly. 'I can't believe your employer lists harassing tourists among your duties.'

'Ah.' He sent her a glance that glinted with amusement. 'But I am not always on duty.' There was a tingling pause, then he turned, and walked to the main door. 'Make your decision, *thespinis*,' he added briskly. 'I am waiting to lock up.'

Biting her lip, she followed him out of the house, and round the terrace to the gate she'd noticed earlier, which he courteously unlatched for her.

'I suggest you come back this way,' he said. 'The track that Stavros' wife uses is rather too steep.'

'Thank you,' Zoe said coldly.

'*Parakalo.*' He grinned at her. 'It has been my pleasure.'

As she descended the steps she was conscious of his gaze following her. Knew the exact moment he turned away, as if a wire joining them had suddenly snapped.

A few minutes later, she heard the sound of a Jeep starting up, and driving away.

Alone at last, she thought. And was shocked to discover her relief tinged by something very like regret.

CHAPTER THREE

I'M MAKING altogether too much of this, Zoe told herself determinedly. He's gone. And it's time I pulled myself together, and forgot about him.

She'd had a wonderful swim, and now, having applied sun lotion to every exposed portion of her skin, she was stretched out on her towel with her book. But she could not concentrate on the printed words. They seemed to dance away out of reach, leaving her to focus almost helplessly on a dark face, with eyes that smiled, looking up at her from the foot of a marble staircase.

In a way it was understandable that he should be imprinted so firmly on her mind. After all, he'd caught her in the act of having a humiliating snoop on private property. He could have handed her over to the police, or even exacted a very different form of retribution, she thought, swallowing.

But she had to put all that behind her now, and plan her next move instead.

I'm here for a purpose, she told herself strongly. And I'm certainly not a lonely heart tourist looking for a holiday romance with some Greek version of Casanova.

Or even a mild flirtation, she made the hasty addendum. Although, to someone like him, it would probably be as natural as breathing. See a woman. Chat her up. Tell her that she's beautiful and desirable. Make her day.

Well, it hasn't made my day, she thought, broodingly.

She sat up, rummaging in her bag for her bottle of water. There wasn't a great deal left, she realised with a frown. She would have to ration herself.

She tossed her book aside, and turned onto her front,

39

undoing the clasp of her bikini top. A little serious sun-bathing, she decided, and then she would go back to the hotel, and sit in the shade with a cold drink.

She pillowed her head on her folded arms, and closed her eyes. The murmur of the sea seemed to fill her head, soothing away the doubts and alarms of the day.

It's just so perfect here, she thought drowsily as everything slid away. It seemed that she was standing in front of Gina's picture, stepping into it like Alice, and entering its world. Retracing her steps in slow motion through every room. Taking a dream-like possession.

She did not fall deeply asleep. She was aware of sand under her fingers, the texture of the towel beneath her bare breasts, and the strength of the sun on her back, like the caress of warm hands. She sighed a little, wriggling her shoulders slowly and pleasurably, then let herself drift again.

Until she found herself once more at the top of the stairs—looking down. Meeting his gaze. And, this time, watching him walk up the steps towards her...

She came back to reality with a sudden jolt, heart thudding. She propped herself up on an elbow, staring around her in sudden, inexplicable alarm, but the rest of the beach was deserted.

She sank back onto the towel with a little groan of relief, then paused, her brows snapping together. Because the bottle of sun lotion that she'd replaced in her bag after use was there in front of her on the sand, propped against an insulated cool-box, which had appeared from nowhere.

Both of them telling her quite clearly that, although she might be alone now, she'd had company quite recently. While she'd been asleep, in fact, and vulnerable.

Her throat tightened as she smelt the distinctive scent of freshly applied lotion on her skin, and remembered the vivid sensation of stroking hands on her bare back. And her drowsy, sensuous reaction...

Oh, God, she thought, he'd been here—touching her.

Seeing her next door to naked. And making no secret of it either. Feverishly, she snatched up her bikini top, and fastened it round her with shaking hands. Locking the stable door, she realised, after the horse was long gone.

He'd said he was leaving, she thought numbly. She'd heard him drive off. And now he'd come sneaking back. All Adele's warnings returned in Technicolor to haunt her. To tell her to get out while the going was good.

She grabbed her bag, and pushed her book and the sun lotion into it. He'd mentioned another way off the beach that Sherry used, and she didn't care how steep or stony it was. It would certainly be safer than going up to the villa, and encountering him again.

Then as she reached for her dress she saw him coming down the steps, a sun umbrella under one arm, and a bottle of water in his other hand. And a towel, she noted, draped round his shoulders.

Too late to run now, she thought, cursing under her breath. She got to her feet, and watched him approach, hands on her hips.

She said glacially, 'I thought you had other duties elsewhere.'

'I also have a lunch break.' He indicated the cool-box, apparently oblivious to the hostility in her tone. 'I thought you might like to share some food with me.'

'Then you thought wrong.' She gave him the full glare that worked so well with stroppy teenagers, both eyes like lasers.

'As you wish.' His own tone was equable. 'But at least drink some of this water I have brought for you. It is dangerous to become dehydrated, and your own supply has nearly gone.'

He pushed the tip of the umbrella he was carrying deep into the sand, and adjusted it, so the shade fell across her towel.

'You dared to go through my things...'

He shrugged. 'I was looking for the lotion to put on your

back. You were in danger of burning. I saw then how little water you had.'

Oh, God, he made it all sound so bloody *reasonable*, she raged inwardly. As if his motives were of the purest.

She said stiffly, 'I'm sure you meant to be kind…'

'Is that what I intended?' He grinned at her. 'Well, maybe. A little. Or, perhaps, I was thinking how angry my employer would be if he found you were in the clinic with first-degree burns or heatstroke, and unable to talk business with him.' He held the bottle of water out to her. 'Now drink some of this.'

'That won't be necessary,' she denied swiftly. 'I'm going back to the hotel. I can get a drink there.'

'I see.' He was quiet for a meditative moment. 'Have you been to Greece many times before?'

'No,' she said. 'This is actually my first visit, but…'

'But it is wiser to rest in the heat of the day,' he supplied decisively. 'And not go walking when there is no necessity.' He put the bottle down on her towel, and paused. 'Don't you like the beach?'

'It's perfect,' Zoe said shortly.

'Until I came to spoil it for you,' he added drily. 'You have a very eloquent face, *thespinis*.'

'Yet you seem determined to stay, all the same.' She observed him spreading his towel on the sand with misgiving.

'I come every day at this time,' he said. 'Whereas you, *thespinis*, are here only at my invitation.' He allowed that to sink in. 'And the beach is surely big enough for us to share for a short while.'

'I'm not sure your employer would agree,' she said tautly. 'Does he know this is how you spend your time?'

'He would certainly consider it one of my duties to offer hospitality to his guest.'

'I am not,' she said. 'His guest. Officially. And you have a very strange idea of hospitality.'

'Why?' His brows lifted. 'I have brought you food, drink

and shelter.' He stood, hands on hips, and looked her up and down slowly, and with unconcealed appreciation, his eyes lingering on the smooth rise of her breasts above the flimsy cups of her bikini. 'But if there is any requirement I have not supplied, you have only to tell me,' he added silkily.

'Thank you,' Zoe said through gritted teeth. 'You've already done more than enough.'

He laughed. 'Then shall we declare a truce, *thespinis*? It is too beautiful a day to fight. And if you won't eat with me, at least drink some water.'

Zoe gave him a mutinous look, then knelt, and carefully decanted some of the water he'd brought into her own container. 'Thank you.' Stonily, she placed the bottle on the outermost corner of the towel, where he had now stretched himself, very much at his ease.

'*Efharisto,*' he corrected, lazily. 'If you are going to stay on the island for any length of time, you need to learn a little Greek.'

'I have a phrase book,' she said. 'So I don't need personal tutoring—thanks.'

His brows drew together. 'You also have attitude,' he told her drily. 'Maybe you could learn, instead, a little *philoxenia*—the Greek warmth towards strangers. Because others may not understand.'

'Perhaps,' Zoe said, lifting her chin coolly, 'this is not a situation where warmth is advisable.'

He propped himself up on one elbow and looked at her measuringly. 'What makes you so nervous?' he asked. 'You think that I intend, maybe, to force myself upon you?' He shook his head. 'No, *thespinis*. In the first place, it is far too hot. In the second, rape has no appeal for me.'

He lay back, looking up at the cloudless sky, lacing his fingers behind his head, his voice meditative.

'I prefer a cool room, with the shutters drawn, a comfortable bed, a bottle of good wine, and a girl who wishes to be with me as much as I want her.'

He turned his head, sending her a faint smile. 'And nothing less will do. So, you see, you are quite safe.'

Her face warmed. She said huskily, 'You paint—a vivid picture.'

'And, I hope, a reassuring one.'

'Yes,' she said. 'Oh, yes.' And tried to subdue the betraying quiver deep inside her.

'Enough to tell me your name?'

She hesitated. 'It's—Zoe.'

'A Greek name,' he approved softly. 'And I am Andreas.' He paused. 'So now that we are properly acquainted, will you share some lunch with me?'

There seemed no good reason to refuse. And perhaps it would be sensible to be a little conciliatory to someone who might be in a position to help her.

So she gave a constrained smile, and murmured, 'That would be—nice.'

The cool-box contained cold chicken, a bag of salad leaves, black olives, tomatoes, feta cheese and some fresh bread. There was also, she noted, a plastic box containing dark grapes and peaches, as well as two chilled bottles of beer, two glasses wrapped in napkins, paper plates, and some cutlery.

This had never been planned as a solitary meal, she thought. And her agreement, it seemed, had been taken for granted. But then he probably didn't get many refusals, she thought, with an inward grimace. And at least he'd brought beer, and not the bottle of good wine he'd mentioned earlier. So attempted seduction did not appear to be on the menu.

It was also clear that she was expected to set out the plates, and divide the food between them. Woman's work, she supposed with irony. And found herself wondering who had assembled the picnic in the first place.

Yet, in spite of her reservations, she enjoyed the meal. The chicken was succulent and the olives and tomatoes had a superb tangy flavour that made those in the supermarket at home seem pallid by comparison.

'Would you like a peach?' He peeled it for her deftly, and she watched his hands, observing the long fingers and well-kept nails. Pretty fastidious for a gardener, she thought. And although his deep voice with its husky timbre was faintly accented, his English seemed faultless.

Andreas, she thought, and wondered…

The fruit was marvellous, too, ripe and sweet, although she was embarrassed to find the juice running down her chin, and into the cleft between her breasts. Something that was not lost on him, she realised with vexation, trying to mop herself discreetly with her napkin.

To deflect his attention, she said, 'Do you like gardening?'

'I enjoy seeing the results,' he said. 'Why? Are you thinking of hiring my services when you come to live at the house?'

She dried her fingers. 'I haven't given it a thought,' she fibbed.

He shrugged a shoulder. 'Then think of it now.'

'Are you so much in demand?'

'Of course,' he said promptly. 'But I could be persuaded to make time for you in my busy schedule.'

He either had the biggest ego in the western world, Zoe told herself seething, or it was a wind-up, and she was sure it was the latter.

But whichever it was, it remained light years away from the taciturn attitude of Mr Harbutt, who wore heavy boots and corduroy trousers summer and winter, and smelled faintly of compost, and who'd done the heavy digging at the cottage for her mother.

She said coolly, 'I think you could prove too expensive for me.'

'You devastate me,' Andreas said lightly. 'Perhaps we could work out a deal together—some kind of reciprocal arrangement.' He watched her stiffen, then went on silkily,

'Much of the island's economy is conducted on the barter system. If you are to live here you will have to accustom yourself.' He paused. 'Tell me, Zoe *mou*, what do you do for a living?'

'I teach,' she said shortly. 'English.'

'Then there is no problem,' he said. 'I will look after your garden. You can give me English lessons.'

Zoe sent him a fulminating look. 'I think your English is quite good enough already.'

His own eyes danced. There were, she noticed unwillingly, tiny gold flecks in their dark depths. 'Thank you,' he said. 'I think.' He sighed elaborately. 'Then we will just have to come up with something else.'

'Or I could simply find another gardener.' She paused. 'But perhaps your boss will refuse to rent the house to me.'

'I do not see how he could resist you, Zoe *mou*. Particularly when I shall give you my strongest endorsement.'

'You think mowing grass and removing weeds gives you special insight into character?' Her brows lifted. 'How fascinating. And your boss will listen to you?'

'He trusts my judgement,' Andreas said slowly. 'When I tell him which plants will grow and thrive, and those that are weak and not worth the trouble. I find human nature is much the same.'

Aghast, she heard herself say, 'And which am I?'

There was a sudden hard edge to his smile. 'When I have come to a decision, Zoe *mou*, I will tell you.'

He collected up the debris from their meal and put it back in the cool-box. Then he stood up, unzipped his shorts unhurriedly, and stepped out of them, revealing brief black swimming trunks, and walked off down the beach.

She felt her mouth dry as she watched him go. He had a miraculous body, she thought, lean, hard and perfectly proportioned. And a long, lithe stride like the prowl of some great cat.

And while the predator was away, the mouse would be wise to make a dash for it, she told herself, swiftly pulling herself together as he plunged into the water and began to swim away, out to sea, with a strong, clean stroke.

She put on her dress, shook out her towel, grabbed her bag and made for the steps. With every yard, she expected to hear him shout after her, or even to feel his hand, damp and salty, on her shoulder halting her. Turning her towards him.

At the top of the steps, Zoe risked one swift look back. His dark head was perfectly visible, his lean body cutting effortlessly through the water. A man in his physical prime enjoying the challenge of tough exercise, and, thankfully, oblivious to her departure.

All the same, once she reached the shade of the olive trees she began to run, pausing only when she reached the road, a hand pressed to her side.

I think, she told herself, her flurried breath hoarse in her throat, that's what they call a lucky escape.

She was hot and sticky by the time she reached the hotel. She collected her key from the hook and went up to her room, guiltily glad that Sherry wasn't around to ask about her day.

By the time she sat down for dinner, she would hopefully be feeling more composed, with some bland comment about Thania's undeniable charm carefully lined up.

Something on the lines of 'Nice island, shame about the natives'? Well, perhaps not, she thought, her mouth twisting.

Or maybe she could make a joke of it all. 'Up at the villa, I ran into the gardener from hell. Who does that guy think he is?' And perhaps Sherry would know, and tell her.

But why did she even want to know?

Because this is a very small island, she thought. And although she intended to avoid the Villa Danae until its supposed owner returned from Athens, she was bound to run into Andreas at some future point, so needed some plan to respond to the situation.

She sighed impatiently. Don't fool yourself, she muttered under her breath. He won't waste any more time on you. You can't be the only female tourist under twenty-five on Thania, and he wants someone warm and willing. He told you so himself.

In the shower, she turned the water to cool, letting it run through her hair and cascade down her overheated body.

It was annoying to contemplate how easily Andreas had been able to get under her skin.

Face it, she thought. You've been out of the mating game too long to know how to deal with someone like that. If you ever knew at all, that is. Dear old George with his bumbling proposal is more your mark, my dear. Not someone who's clearly been sex on legs since the day he was born.

She towelled herself dry, and put on her thin silk wrap, then helped herself to a can of lemonade from the minifridge in the corner, and took it out onto the balcony with the papers for the Villa Danae.

What she needed was someone to verify the translation of the original document gifting the villa to her mother. She supposed she could ask Stavros, but the gift was clearly the action of a rich man, and she remembered what Sherry had said about her husband not wishing to offend any of the influential residents on Thania.

She also had to find out the identity of Andreas' employer in Athens. If she hadn't been caught totally on the wrong foot, she would have asked. But being caught in the villa had thrown her mental processes into turmoil.

And her emotions had followed, she thought, biting savagely at her lower lip.

Andreas had knocked her sideways, in a way that was completely foreign to her nature, and it was pointless to deny it. Thank God her instinct for self-preservation had still been working, she thought, shifting restlessly in the cushioned chair.

And anyway, she'd had enough sun for one day. Against

the concealing silk, her skin felt warm, but not burning. And for that, she supposed, moving her shoulders experimentally, she had to thank Andreas' ministrations with the sun lotion.

She could still feel the glide of his hands on her back, and yet with Mick, who'd been her only lover to date, she could not remember a single detail of their intimacy.

I shouldn't be able to remember Andreas' touch like this, she thought almost frantically. I was asleep, for God's sake.

But if you hadn't gone on sleeping, said a small, sly voice in her head. If you'd woken, what would you have done? Would you have lain still, pretending? Or would you have turned over, offering your bare breasts? Drawing him down to you, because you could not help yourself?

She felt her throat tighten uncontrollably. Her breathing quicken.

This, she told herself forcefully, is not good. Don't even go there.

Nothing had happened. Nothing was going to happen. But she would have to watch every step she took from now on.

I had no idea, she thought drearily, fanning herself with the papers, that I could be so susceptible.

The ferry was just leaving, and for a moment she almost wished she were on it.

I really shouldn't have come here, she thought, frowning. Not without knowing the score in advance. And I certainly shouldn't have betrayed my interest in the house so soon. But what real choice did I have between that, and being hauled off by the local police for trespass?

She sighed again, ruefully. It was all just an unfortunate combination of circumstances.

But from now, I'll cool it, she told herself. Sherry is bound to know when Andreas' boss returns from Athens, and I'll make sure I keep any questions casual and discreet.

And if I happen to meet Andreas again in the meantime, I'll let him think that I was simply winding him up in turn.

Trying to get myself out of a tight spot with a few well-chosen fibs.

That was the best—the only way to handle things. For all kinds of reasons, she thought, of which her own peace of mind was only one.

'Did you find the beach all right?' Sherry asked that evening, setting a dish of taramasalata on Zoe's table.

'Oh, yes.' Zoe allowed herself a wry smile and a shrug. 'Only it wasn't quite as deserted as you said.'

'Oh, heck.' Sherry wrinkled her nose. 'Is Steve Dragos back? I hadn't realised. I thought he was still wrapped in cotton wool in Athens after his heart attack.'

'I don't think the guy I met is a candidate for heart trouble,' Zoe said. Although he might cause his fair share of it, she added silently. 'He seemed to be some sort of gardener-caretaker.'

'Really?' Sherry looked surprised. 'I didn't know there was one. Maybe he's some relation to Hara who looks after the house. What's his name?'

'I'm not sure he mentioned it,' Zoe said untruthfully, filling her glass with water. It had occurred to her suddenly that she didn't want to have all her prejudices about Andreas confirmed. To be told by Sherry that his bed was collapsing from all the notches in its post. Or even to be teased about her encounter with him. 'So,' she went on. 'Who is this Steve Dragos?'

'Oh your usual multimillionaire.' Sherry shrugged. 'Runs fleets of tankers and freight carriers round the world. And somehow, in between it all, found the time to build the Villa Danae.'

'Heavens,' said Zoe, rather faintly. 'I—see.' She paused. 'Yet he doesn't live there.'

'Oh, no. He has an even more palatial villa just up the coast.' Sherry gave her an anxious look as she unloaded from her tray the small carafe of white house wine that Zoe had ordered. 'I hope you didn't get into trouble for being there,' she added quietly.

'No, it was fine,' Zoe assured her. She lowered her voice in turn. 'But they know you use the beach sometimes.'

'Hell,' Sherry said gloomily. 'Steve Dragos must have a spy camera up on some satellite. Thank God I'm not into skinny-dipping.' And she went off to take the order from a German family at an adjoining table.

Zoe had a lot to think about as she ate her grilled swordfish, and its accompanying salad. Was the man in the photograph this Steve Dragos—and had he given the Villa Danae to her mother? And, if so—why?

What on earth had Gina Lambert been doing mixing in that kind of super-wealthy society? It made no sense. Family life had been comfortable, but there was little money to spare. And certainly no indication from her mother that she'd once moved with the jet set.

She had the uneasy feeling that she was getting into deep water, but she couldn't back off now. She needed desperately to know everything.

Her sense of disquiet was also heightened to simmering point by the expectation of seeing Andreas walk into the courtyard at any moment. After all, he knew where she was staying, and she'd been secretly convinced he would come to find her, if only to make some edged remark about her ignominious retreat. On the other hand, maybe he'd decided to shrug her off as the one that got away. Because that had been her intention—hadn't it?

All the same, every new arrival sent her heart thumping, but there was no tall, arrogant figure scanning the tables with narrowed dark eyes.

Her hasty departure seemed to have had the desired effect, she thought. She should be grateful for that, and she knew it.

Every glance, every smile he'd sent her had revealed the practised womaniser, she told herself. And his relationships would be just as fragile and ephemeral as any of the butterflies with wings like chocolate velvet that she'd seen in the garden at the villa. Which was the last thing she needed.

She ate her dessert of fresh apricots, and lingered over the coffee and Metaxa that rounded off the meal.

'That was wonderful,' she sighed when Sherry came to clear the table. 'My compliments to the chef.'

'That's my mother-in-law,' Sherry told her cheerfully. 'The most unflappable woman in the universe. And a great dancer, too. You'll see her in action tomorrow night when we have live music.'

All the other diners were leaving, most of them to walk along the harbourside and find a taverna for a final nightcap. Zoe supposed she could do the same, but instead she found herself going back to her room.

It's been quite a day, she thought, and a comparatively early night will do me no harm at all.

Besides, it was unexpectedly lonely being on one's own in a foreign country, where other people all seemed to be couples or family groups.

Had Gina been lonely, too, and tempted, as a result, away from the normal pattern of her existence? Was that what this was all about—a holiday fling with a man, who turned out to be rich enough to give houses as farewell presents instead of the conventional piece of jewellery?

It wasn't a very palatable possibility, she thought, opening her door. But it made sense.

As she switched on the light, she glimpsed herself in the wall-mirror, a girl with pale hair and wide, expectant eyes in a black slip of a dress cut low across her breasts. A dress to please a man, she thought with sudden self-contempt. In spite of everything she'd told herself that afternoon.

Maybe this was how it had begun for her mother, too. Perhaps Gina had stood in a room like this one, feeling the stir of sheer physical attraction along her senses. Finding it irresistible.

Had she stayed here, and fought for her self-respect, or had she gone back, flitting like a slender ghost, to where he'd been waiting for her in the shadow of the cypress trees?

But Andreas was not waiting anywhere for her, she reminded herself. His work was over for the day, and he was probably at home in some small white house in Livassi, with a wife and brood of children.

She made a sound in her throat, muffled, painful.

I walked away, she thought. I behaved well. I did the right thing. The only thing.

So why do I feel as if I lost?

CHAPTER FOUR

ZOE slept badly, and was wide awake in time to see the sun rise in a flawless sky, promising another intensely hot day.

She'd had time, during the night, to decide her next move, so she showered and dressed in a knee-length black linen skirt, with a matching vest top over her bikini. Her hair she twisted into a loose knot on top of her head secured by a silver clasp.

'Not going back to the cove?' Sherry asked, pouring breakfast coffee into her cup.

'I think that would be pushing my luck an inch too far,' Zoe admitted with utter truth, at the same time stifling a pang of totally unsuitable regret. 'I thought I'd do some sightseeing instead, before it gets too warm. Discover what Livassi has to offer.' *And, maybe, meet Uncle Stavros…*

'Well, don't blink,' Sherry advised. 'Or you might miss it.' Then, relenting, 'Actually, Livassi's really pretty, and the church is lovely with some terrific frescos. But they like you to cover your shoulders if you plan to visit.'

'I've got a shirt to put on.' Zoe delved into her bag, and produced it, checked in black and white, with long sleeves, and voluminous enough to wear as a beach cover-up later.

'And watch out for the icon,' Sherry added as she turned away. 'It's supposed to help women get pregnant so you might want to give it a wide berth.'

'That's OK.' Zoe tried a nonchalant shrug. 'I'm totally celibate.'

'That's what they all say,' said Sherry darkly.

And that, thought Zoe, is what I have to believe, and keep to. At all costs.

The hill up to the main square was steep, and narrow enough to force her to leap into doorways as cars and scooters roared heedlessly past.

By the time she reached the top, she was hot and breathless, but she had to admit that the square with its Venetian-style colonnade and small Byzantine church was well worth the effort.

There were tables in the middle of the square under the trees, and benches, but, as yet, they were unoccupied. Perhaps the games of backgammon didn't take place at weekends, she reflected, disappointed. Well, there would be other days.

She took some photographs, then, pulling on her shirt, went into the cool, incense-laden atmosphere of the church. A bearded priest in dark robes replacing candles in tall holders gave her a lightning glance, then made her a slight bow of unsmiling approval.

She trod round slowly, her sandals noiseless on the stone flags, looking at the murals that depicted scenes from the life of Christ, which she recognised, and various angular, wistful-eyed saints, which she didn't.

There were numerous icons in niches round the walls, all of them apparently venerated, so she had no idea which one to avoid.

In any case, she thought, her mouth twisting, it was a real man she needed to shun, not a gilded representation painted on wood.

The heat was like a blow from a clenched fist as she emerged into the sunlight. She ordered an iced drink made from fresh lemons at a *kafeneion* under the colonnade, and settled down under its striped awning to look around her.

One of the tables under the trees was occupied now by a group of elderly men hunched round a board, their hands moving with incredible speed as they threw dice and moved counters. But which of them, if any, was Uncle Stavros? And she could hardly interrupt their concentration in order to ask, she decided wryly.

She retrieved from her bag the small guide book she'd bought on her way up the hill, and began to flick through it.

But apart from extolling the wondrous peace and quiet of the island, and the fact that it was used as a retreat by some of the rich and famous, there was not a great deal the author could say.

There was a bay where Odysseus might or might not have paused for breath on the last leg of his epic journey back to Ithaca, and which bore his name on the off chance. There was a ruined monastery, and a couple of tiny fishing villages with wonderful views over the Ionian Sea. There were any number of walks, none of which would take more than a few hours to complete, including one up the steep slopes of Mount Edira, with even more breathtaking views.

And there were the Silver Caves. These, she read, were situated on the other side of the island, and led to a small subterranean lake. Some mineral in the rock gave it a metallic sheen, and affected the colour of the water, too, hence the name. Boats could be hired to row across the lake, and at night, when moonlight penetrated a fissure in the roof, visitors would feel they were enclosed in a precious silver casket.

Not for the claustrophobic then, Zoe thought drily, but she had to admit it sounded appealing.

There was also an echo in the caves, which had been used for generations on the island by lovers to test the fidelity of their chosen partners. If you called the loved one's name, and it echoed back, then you had nothing to fear. But if there was silence…

Hideous embarrassment all round, thought Zoe, entertained.

As she closed the book she was suddenly aware that she was being watched.

She glanced up and met the frowning gaze of a newcomer to the backgammon game. He was solidly built, with a mass of silver hair under a rakish peaked cap, his once handsome face heavily lined. His hands were clasped in front of him on top of a walking stick.

Even when Zoe met his eye, he did not look away, but went on staring at her curiously, almost fiercely, as if he knew her, but was cursing the fact that he could not place her.

But I bet I know who you are, Zoe told herself silently. *Kalimera*, Uncle Stavros.

She had half risen from her chair with the intention of going over to speak to him when he rose and moved away, walking quickly for a man leaning heavily on a stick.

Zoe sank back, feeling oddly deflated. She knew from photographs how closely she resembled her mother at the same age.

It was clear he'd picked up the family resemblance, she thought flatly, but he hadn't wanted to renew the acquaintance. Nor had he wished to be questioned about it.

Well, this is only the third day of my vacation, she thought. There's plenty of time ahead for his curiosity to get the better of him. And I'm sure it will.

If not, I'll make the first approach myself.

She looked rather defensively at the backgammon players, but they were totally absorbed in their game. None of them had a second glance to spare for her.

Ah, well—investigation over for today, she thought, leaving the money on the table for the waiter. And back to being a tourist again.

But all the way down the hill she found herself remembering that concentrated, almost worried stare, and wondering…

Sherry, reflected Zoe, had not been joking about the town beach getting busy. She was beginning to know how a sardine had to feel as the tin closed round it, and it wasn't even noon yet, she thought, groaning.

It seemed the entire population of Livassi had turned out to sun themselves, and bathe in the shallow water. Or play something like volleyball without the net, she thought without pleasure as a large beach ball thudded down beside her, yet again, spraying her with fine sand.

The young Greek who ran over to retrieve it gave her a flashing smile that bordered on a leer, while his friends shouted something that might have been encouragement.

'Hey, pretty girl, you want to play?' he demanded.

'No, thank you,' Zoe returned austerely, adding a muted glare, then transferred her attention ostentatiously back to the book she was reading.

There were four of them altogether, and they'd been a nuisance ever since they arrived. And because she was a girl on her own, they seemed to have singled her out for special attention, she realised with growing annoyance. The ball was being deliberately batted in her direction, so that they could come rushing over in turn, strutting their stuff, bending far too close, and making grinning remarks that she was grateful not to understand. Until now, when they'd worked out that she was English rather than German or Swedish as they'd probably assumed.

For the first time, she regretted being alone, realising that it made her conspicuous, and a sitting target for the local Romeos.

She looked surreptitiously around, hoping to see one of the families who were also staying at the hotel, but everyone around her seemed to be Greek. And, anyway, she was probably fussing too much about a bit of innocent horseplay, she told herself, and eventually, when she didn't respond, they'd get bored and stop.

But ten minutes later, when she was still being regularly spattered with sand, she decided to cut her losses, and go.

It wasn't really such a hardship, she told herself. It was lunchtime, and she could try the fish taverna she'd passed on the harbourside. Perhaps by the time she came back they would either have moved on, or found some other female to pester.

She slipped her check shirt over her bikini, fastening the

middle buttons, then collected her things and stood up. She'd hoped they were too immersed in their game to notice, but by the time she reached the stony track bordering the beach that led back to the harbour, she realised to her alarm that two of them were following her.

She quickened her pace, stumbling a little as the loose pebbles on the track rolled under her sandalled feet, and the stocky one who had spoken to her in English caught up with her effortlessly, putting a hand on her arm.

'You come—have drink in my brother's bar?' He grinned at her, his eyes insolent, as he looked her up and down.

'No, thank you.' Zoe's response was cold and unsmiling. She tried to tug herself free, but to no avail. His hand closed on her more firmly.

'We want you to be friendly.' His companion came to her other side, so that she was effectively trapped between them. 'I work on Zakynthos last year.' He rolled his eyes lasciviously. 'All English girls very friendly.'

'You have apartment?' the first one asked. 'We go there—have drink maybe, *kougla mou*. Is quieter—more private.' He pushed up her sleeve, stroking the skin on the inside of her arm with hot, damp fingers.

Zoe's anger began to give way to something like fear. But she dared not show it.

She said furiously, 'Let go of me. Let go at once.'

The second youth laughed, showing a broken tooth. 'Be nice, honey girl, and we show you a good time.'

'And I,' said Zoe, 'will show you the inside of a jail cell.'

With a strength she'd not known she possessed, she wrenched herself loose and set off, running. But before she'd gone more than a few yards she cannoned into someone who was standing, blocking her way, and recoiled with a scream.

'Hush, *pedhi mou*.' It was Andreas' voice. His hands

descended firmly on her shoulders, holding her. 'All is well. You are safe.'

He looked past her to her assailants, speaking softly in his own language.

Zoe saw with disbelief that all the macho bluster and posturing had suddenly gone out of them, just as if someone had thrown a switch. They were staring at the ground, muttering and shrugging, looking hangdog, and almost embarrassed. Then, as Andreas spoke more sharply, they turned and slouched away back to the beach.

'My God.' Her voice was shaky. 'They didn't put up much of a fight.'

His brows lifted. 'You would like me to call them back, perhaps.'

'No—oh, no.' She paused. 'What did you say to them to make them—disappear like that? Do they know you?'

'Of course,' he said. 'Thania is a very small island. And, among other things, I reminded them that we all work for the same man, who would not be pleased to find them accused of sexually harassing a tourist. Although I have to tell you that they are both more stupid than dangerous.'

'Not,' Zoe said, 'from where I was sitting.' She took a deliberate step away from him, releasing herself from his grasp, and gave him a frowning look. He was wearing denim trousers, and his thin white shirt was unbuttoned, revealing, once again, more smooth brown skin than she wished to see. She hurried into speech. 'Is that all you said to them?'

'There were embellishments,' he said. 'But I will not trouble you with those.'

'Oh.' She digested that, then looked at him with renewed suspicion. 'Anyway, what are you doing here?'

'I thought—rescuing you from annoyance.'

She brushed that aside impatiently. 'I mean—how did you happen to be here just in the nick of time? Isn't that rather a strange coincidence?'

'Ah,' Andreas said softly. 'A conspiracy theory. But

there is no need for paranoia, *pedhi mou*. Or to imagine that I hired those idiots to annoy you, so that I could play the part of some knight in shining armour,' he added. 'You needed help, and I happened to come along. That is all.'

'You just *happened* to be here?'

He shrugged. 'This is a public path, leading to a public beach,' he countered. 'Why should I not be here?' He paused. 'Although I admit I was coming to look for you.'

Her already flustered heartbeat began to pound to a different rhythm. 'Why should you do that?'

And why did I ask that, she wondered despairingly, when I don't want to hear the answer?

'Because the beach at the house seemed quiet without you.' He smiled at her. 'And yesterday you left without saying goodbye.'

Zoe stared down at the dusty track. 'I felt embarrassed,' she said in a low voice. 'An intruder. I—I had no real right to be there, and I knew it.'

'Even though I had made it clear you were a welcome guest?'

'Well, it was hardly your place to do that,' she returned. 'However strict he is about hassling women tourists, your boss might not appreciate your entertaining visitors in his absence.'

'I promise you he would feel honoured.'

She hunched a shoulder. 'All the same, I think it would be better to keep my distance from now on.'

He frowned slightly. 'So the house no longer interests you?' he queried. 'You have changed your mind about wishing to live there.'

'I didn't say that.'

'Good,' he said. 'Because I have told my employer of your interest, and he is looking forward to meeting you.'

She drew a swift, astonished breath. She hadn't expected that. She'd intended to make her own enquiries—stay in control of the situation, yet now it seemed to be taken out of her hands.

'Isn't that a little premature?' It was her turn to frown. 'I gather he's been very ill.'

'He is on the mend. Also bored. He needs entertainment—a new interest, which you could provide.'

'I want to discuss business with him,' Zoe said shortly. 'I'm not a cabaret act.'

'No,' he said, silkily. 'They tend to smile more.'

She bit her lip. 'I'm—sorry. I'm still rather stressed, I think.'

'You need food,' he said. 'And a glass of wine. So, have lunch with me, and over the meal you can express your gratitude to me for coming to your aid, as I am sure you wish to do.'

Zoe felt her jaw begin to drop, and restored it hurriedly to its correct position. Somehow, he'd wrong-footed her again. How on earth did he do that?

Not that it altered a thing. She wasn't prepared to venture on another meal *à deux* with him, even if there was a table between them, and loads of other people around this time. It was too dangerous. Her reaction to him was too extreme. As it was, she was shaking inside.

She managed a small cool smile. 'I already have plans for lunch,' she said. 'So I'd better say thanks here and now. You saved me from a—nasty situation, and I am grateful. Truly.' She contemplated offering to shake hands with him, and decided against it. 'So, thank you again and—see you around.'

She walked away, trying not to hurry, and certainly not risking even a glance over her shoulder to see how he had taken his rejection. Surely by now he'd have got the message, she argued with herself. Besides, remembering the prices she'd checked on the menus displayed outside the fish taverna earlier, she'd be doing him a favour. He couldn't afford them on a gardener's wage.

The taverna was crowded, nearly all the tables being occupied, and Zoe was hesitating at the entrance, wondering whether to return another day instead, when a smiling waiter materialised beside her. 'You want good fish. Come, please. I have a nice table for you.'

He whisked her under the green awning to a secluded spot in the corner, shaded by a flowering vine growing up a trellis.

Nice, thought Zoe, sinking into her chair with an inner sigh of contentment, was not the word.

She reached out a hand and touched the petals on the small jar of golden rosebuds occupying the centre of the snowy cloth, then paused as a swift glance around her revealed that hers was the only table with such a decoration.

The waiter came bustling back, bringing chilled water and a basket containing crusty bread and, she realised with growing unease, two sets of cutlery.

She began, 'Excuse me…' but he was off, weaving his way among the tables to return a moment later with an ice bucket and a bottle of white wine.

This time, Zoe pushed back her chair with determination. 'I'm sorry,' she said. 'There's obviously been some mistake.'

'No,' Andreas said. 'No mistake at all.' And he slid almost casually into the chair opposite and smiled at her. 'I hope you are hungry. Kostas has lobster for us.'

She sat, frozen in fury, staring at him, while the waiter filled their glasses. As soon as he'd departed, she leaned forward. 'Let's get one thing straight,' she said in an icy undertone. 'There is no "us".'

'No?' His brows lifted mockingly. 'Yet all it takes is for two people to be together—and we are certainly that.'

'And just how did this togetherness come about?' Zoe demanded. 'How did you know where I was planning to eat? Or did you book tables in every taverna in town?'

He shrugged. 'Sooner or later, everyone comes to eat at Kostas' taverna. I thought you would like it here, and took a chance.'

'Well, it hasn't paid off,' she flung at him. 'I'm going.'

'You don't like lobster?'

'This has nothing to do with food.' She rose. 'I don't like being second-guessed and manipulated. Particularly when I'd made it clear I was lunching alone.'

He said meditatively, 'That word "alone" again.' He paused. 'Tell me, *pedhi mou*, do you know what "Zoe" means in Greek?'

'No,' she denied curtly.

The dark eyes met hers, held them. 'It means life,' he said. 'So—how can you be so afraid to live?'

Colour rushed into her face. 'That's a vile thing to say. And totally untrue.'

The dark eyes raked her harshly. 'Then why do you reject friendship when it is offered?'

'Friendship?' she asked bitterly. 'Is that what your colleagues had in mind just now?'

'You believe that I am like them?' His tone was incredulous.

She looked down at the table. 'How do I know?' Her voice was muffled. 'How can I possibly tell? We only met yesterday. We're barely acquaintances.'

'That is something I am trying to change,' he said. 'But not with any great success. Sit down, Zoe *mou*, and I will tell you anything you wish to know.'

'Besides,' he added gently as she hesitated, 'Kostas will be sad if we waste his wonderful lobster.'

Mutinously, Zoe resumed her seat. 'I don't know why I'm doing this,' she muttered.

'Because you're hungry,' Andreas said promptly. 'Also thirsty.' He lifted his glass. 'To your eyes, *agapi mou*.'

Startled by the intimacy of the toast, and conscious that she was blushing, Zoe reluctantly touched her glass to his. 'Cheers,' she said awkwardly.

The waiter reappeared with dishes of houmous and tzatziki, a bowl of black olives and a platter of mixed salad.

'You like Greek food?' Andreas proffered the bread.

'Everything I've had so far has been wonderful.'

'That is just as well,' he said drily. 'On Thania, you will

find little else. No fast food or English pubs,' he added with a touch of grimness.

'Aren't they a fact of life in holiday resorts?'

'On other islands, perhaps.' He sounded quietly certain. 'But not here. We do not wish to go down that road. Thania belongs to its islanders. They fish, and grow their olives and make their wine, and are content with that.'

'And sometimes they garden for rich men,' Zoe said. She tore off a piece of bread and dipped it into the tzatziki. 'Will that make you happy for the rest of your life?'

'Probably not,' he said. 'But gardening is only part of my duties, as I told you, Zoe *mou*.' He smiled at her. 'And I enjoy variety.'

'I bet,' Zoe said under her breath.

His smile widened into a grin, leaving her with the uncomfortable feeling that he knew exactly what she was thinking. 'And what of you, *pedhi mou*? Do you plan to teach English for ever?'

She shrugged a touch defensively. 'Probably.'

He said softly, 'But what a waste. You are not tempted to marry—have children of your own?'

She was assailed by a sudden memory of George doggedly proposing to her in the wine bar, and bit down a giggle.

She met his gaze squarely. 'Not in the slightest. I have a very fulfilling career.'

His brows lifted. 'So, it also keeps you warm in bed at night?'

She flushed again. 'I don't think that's any of your damned business. And I thought the point of this lunch was for me to find out about *you*.'

'Ask what you want,' he said. 'I am ready to answer.'

'Well, your second name might be a start.' She tried to sound casual, not easy when her nerves seemed to be stretched on wires.

Oh, what's the matter with me? she wondered savagely. Any other single girl on holiday would relish being chatted up by someone with half his attraction and sheer charisma. And any of my students would make a better fist of responding than I'm doing. Why can't I just—go with the flow?

'My second name is Stephanos,' he said. 'Andreas Stephanos.' He paused. 'What next, Zoe *mou*? My age—weight—height?'

She bit her lip. 'I hardly think that's necessary.'

Besides, she thought, she already knew what there was to know in that area. Every quivering sense she possessed had made sure of that. He had to be in his early thirties, at least six foot, if not more, and she would bet good money that he wasn't carrying a surplus pound.

'Then what else?' He leaned back in his chair, watching her with amusement. 'My star sign—my income?'

She shrugged again. 'For the first, I'd say Scorpio. The second doesn't concern me.'

He sent her an ironic look. 'Then you must be a very unusual woman.'

'I think so.' She paused. 'Was I right about your birthday?'

His mouth twisted wryly. 'As it happens—yes.' He poured some more wine into her glass. 'So, why don't you ask another question?'

'Because I can't think of one,' she said baldly.

'No? You don't want to know if I'm married?'

She helped herself to more houmous while she considered how to reply. At last she said, 'I'm not sure I should get a truthful answer.'

'What point would there be in lying?' Andreas asked flatly. 'On an island this size, someone would soon tell you if I had a wife.' He grimaced. 'Probably the wife herself—using her fingernails.' He was silent for a moment. 'And what of yourself, Zoe *mou*. You wear no ring, but that means little in this present world. Is there a man longing for your return? Unable to sleep because you are not in his arms?'

'Oh, there's a whole string of them,' she told him airily. 'I'm the original party girl. Never a dull moment with me around.'

'Now that I can believe,' he said, drily. 'But not the rest.'

She drew a pattern on the tablecloth with the tip of her finger. 'I haven't had much time for relationships lately. My mother became very ill, you see, and I went to live with her.'

'I am sorry.' He hesitated. 'She's better now, I hope?'

Zoe went on looking down at the tablecloth, tracing meaningless circles. She gave a silent and desolate shake of her head.

'Ah, *pedhi mou*,' he said, and his voice was gentle. 'Then that is something we share—the loss of our mothers.'

'Oh.' She glanced up quickly, meeting his gaze. 'I—I'm sorry. Did it happen recently?'

'Ten years ago. And she had been in poor health for a very long time before that.' He paused. 'But when it happens, it is still no easy thing, *ne*?'

'Not easy at all.' She gave a small sigh. 'Do you still have your father?'

'Yes.' His mouth curved faintly. 'Very much so.' He gave her a searching look. 'But not you, I think.'

'No,' she said in a stifled tone. 'So now I have to make another life for myself. And this holiday is just its beginning.'

He put a hand over hers, stilling the restless movement. 'Is this why you wish to be alone?' he asked quietly. 'Because you think that if you shut everyone out of this new life of yours, then you will suffer no more pain?' He shook his head. 'It does not work like that, I promise you. Sooner or later, someone will come into your world, and whether they bring heaven or hell, you will not be able to deny yourself.'

She looked down at the long brown fingers covering hers. And felt her whole body clench in sudden yearning.

Hastily, she withdrew her hand, making a business of taking more bread, filling her plate with salad and olives.

She said lightly, 'You make it sound rather frightening—and I've had enough scares for one day.'

'Well, they are over now,' he said. 'And no one else on Thania will make you afraid. I guarantee that.'

Zoe gave him a sceptical look. 'You really have such influence?' She kept her tone light.

'I am known as a man who keeps his word.' He sounded equally casual but she believed him.

'Then it's lucky I ran into you,' she said.

'Not luck, *matia mou*,' Andreas said softly. 'Fate. And here comes our lunch,' he added prosaically as Zoe stared at him, the breath suddenly catching in her throat.

The lobsters were wonderful, served plain grilled, with a dish of melted butter, and another containing a rich pink sauce made from the coral.

And it was impossible, Zoe found, to stay aloof, as she knew she needed to do, during such an informal, messy meal, with Andreas showing her, laughing, how to crack even the tiniest claws and extract every last delicious scrap of meat.

Afterwards, there was a platter of cherries, their creamy skins just flushed with red, and tiny cups of thick Greek coffee served with brandy.

'I don't think I can move,' Zoe confessed.

Andreas smiled at her lazily. 'Then don't do so, *pedhi mou*,' he advised. 'There is no hurry.'

One glance around her told her that he was right. After the earlier buzz, an air of somnolence had settled over the taverna. Most of the customers seemed content to settle back in the shade and let the afternoon pass. Even the voices were hushed. Those drifting away were mostly couples, she realised, and she found herself remembering, with a shiver of awareness, what Andreas had said to her about cool shuttered rooms in the heat of the afternoon. And wondered if he was remembering, too.

'I—I suppose not,' she said, trying to maintain her composure. 'But I'm sure you have places to go, and things to do.' *And people to see...*

He had said he wasn't married, she thought, but there could still be a woman or several in his life. He'd probably been fighting them off, but not too hard, since puberty.

He shrugged. 'They can also wait.' His half smile was wry. 'Unless you want to be rid of me.'

'Of course not.' Well, it was partly true, she thought. Common sense and recklessness were fighting it out in her head. 'And you've been very kind,' she added hastily. 'It's just that I feel I've taken up quite enough of your time.'

He gave her a slow, heavy-lidded glance. 'You think I am merely being kind, Zoe *mou*?' he drawled. 'Are you really so naive?'

'I'm not naive at all,' Zoe said jerkily. 'I was actually giving you the benefit of the doubt. But I see I was wrong.' She reached for her bag. 'And I'd like to pay for my own lunch.'

'You are wasting your time,' Andreas told her, unruffled. 'Kostas will not take your money.'

She lifted her chin. 'Why not?'

He leaned forward, looking into her eyes. He had amazing eyelashes, she found herself thinking inconsequentially, long, thick and curling. Astonishing on someone so completely and disturbingly male.

'For the same reason that you may pursue your quest for solitude on the town beach this afternoon, if you wish,' he told her softly. 'Because you have been with me, and, by this time, it will be known. Which makes you safe from all annoyance.'

Zoe pushed back her chair and rose. She was trembling again, but this time with anger at his sheer presumption.

'Except yours, I assume.' Her voice bit. 'And that's hardly reassuring. But I don't choose to be patronised, and I certainly shan't be going back to the town beach. There must be a corner of this island where your reputation doesn't carry, and I intend to find it, and spend the rest of my holiday in peace.'

'Peace?' he echoed derisively, getting to his feet in turn. 'You forfeited all hope of that when you came to the villa yesterday. And you know that as well as I do, my girl, so don't look at me with those innocent, injured eyes.'

Zoe drew herself up. 'Given the choice,' she said with icy clarity, 'I won't be looking at you at all.'

And she turned and walked out of the taverna, and along the harbourside to the questionable sanctuary of the hotel.

CHAPTER FIVE

'A LUCKY escape.' That's what Zoe kept telling herself, over and over again, as she lay on the bed staring up at the ceiling. And that was what she had to think. Because anything else was impossible.

Having lunch with Andreas Stephanos had been one of the biggest mistakes of her life, and she was ashamed to think how spinelessly she'd succumbed to his invitation.

And also, she realised, wincing, how much she'd enjoyed herself.

But the worst thing of all, she thought broodingly, was the way she'd found herself watching the lurking smile in his dark eyes, and the sensuous curve of the firm mouth. Feeling, as she did so, the muscles of her throat tighten in unfamiliar excitement.

There was no denying that Andreas Stephanos was a dangerously attractive man, and it was only his shameless suggestion that everyone on the island now regarded her as his personal property that had brought her to her senses at last. Before it was too late.

What she could not understand was how he'd managed to acquire such power over his fellow islanders. Was it the influence he seemed to possess with his rich boss, or sheer force of personality? Probably a combination of both, she thought.

Whatever, he was someone she seriously needed to avoid.

She'd been hot and breathless when she got back to the hotel, her legs shaking under her. Her first act had been to take a cool shower, but it had not had the calming effect she'd hoped for.

The thin wrap she was wearing seemed to grate unbearably against her sensitised skin, and there was a deep trembling ache inside her that she found she was unable to dispel.

'Ridiculous,' she told herself forcefully. 'Ludicrous, in fact.'

She'd always regarded herself as being reasonably levelheaded. So how could she explain this totally overheated reaction to a man she'd met twice, and in whose company she'd spent little more than a couple of brief hours?

I just don't do things like this, Zoe thought fretfully, turning over and burying her face in the flat, hard pillow. And, anyway, it's not what I'm here for. I have a serious purpose, and I won't allow myself to forget it.

But the Villa Danae would have to be forbidden territory from now on, or at least until she had the chance to talk to the unknown Steve Dragos, and find out what possible connection he'd had with her mother. And, even then, because of his recent ill health, she would need to tread carefully.

Or she could simply let sleeping dogs lie, she thought restively. Abandon the whole thing, and get her holiday company to book her an earlier return flight. Let the past keep its secrets, and concentrate on the future. In many ways that was a much more appealing alternative.

Except that Gina Lambert's painting would still be there waiting for her—a constant reminder that there was a mystery still unsolved. And that she'd let a golden opportunity slip by. Besides, running away wasn't her style, whatever the provocation.

No, it was better to stay here, she decided with renewed determination. Get things sorted once and for all, whatever the outcome.

And let Andreas Stephanos see that she was one tourist who was immune to the undoubted lure of his physicality.

But if that was the case, asked a sly voice in her brain, why didn't she simply exclude him from the equation altogether? Relegate him to some mental and emotional dumpbin as she'd done with Mick, and poor George?

Because it's not as simple as that, she thought forlornly. And no amount of wishing will make it so.

And the implications of that kept her tossing restlessly until it was time to put on her silky slip of a black dress, do her face and hair, and go down for dinner.

'So, how was the grand tour of Livassi?' Sherry asked as she poured Zoe a retsina.

'I thought it was delightful,' Zoe said with sincerity. 'Even down to the backgammon players.'

Sherry's eyes twinkled. 'Did you meet Uncle Stavros?'

Zoe paused, weighing her words. 'I think he was just leaving as I got there,' she said neutrally. No need to mention, she thought, that her arrival seemed to have driven him to instant retreat.

'Not like him to miss out on an attractive blonde,' Sherry commented cheerfully. 'He must be feeling his age at last.'

Zoe shrugged with a smile. 'Perhaps,' she said, and reached down a foot from her stool in the small tiled bar area to scratch gently an ecstatic Archimedes who was sprawling beside her.

Other guests began to drift in and Sherry went off to serve them.

Zoe sipped her wine, enjoying its distinctive resinated flavour. Sherry's comment about old Stavros seemed to confirm her own impression, she thought. But she wasn't just any blonde. She was her mother's daughter, and he'd picked up on the resemblance, and been disturbed by it. Well, she'd go back to the square tomorrow, and if he tried to disappear again she would follow, and ask a few pertinent questions. Find out what he knew about Gina, and her time on Thania. Because there had to be something.

From the courtyard, she could hear the sound of musicians tuning up, and remembered that Sherry had said there would be dancing.

Time to stop pondering, and start enjoying instead, she told herself. She had a leisurely dinner of lamb, baked in the oven with tomatoes and herbs, accompanied by fried potatoes, green beans, and a full-bodied red wine, and savoured every mouthful.

There were extra tables and chairs tonight, she noticed, and these were rapidly being filled up by local people. Clearly, the Saturday dance at the Hotel Stavros was a real social event, but attended, she saw with relief, mainly by large family groups.

It began with a short display by two young couples in traditional local dress, who began threading their way between the tables, encouraging the hotel guests to join them in a long chain. When they reached Zoe, she shook her head with a smile. She'd never been much of a dancer, she thought wryly, and she was frankly deterred, anyway, by the intricacy of the steps.

It was pleasant to sit in her corner, drinking wine, and listening to the faintly oriental sound of the bouzouki players. She was clapping to the rhythm, her attention concentrated on the dancers, now moving in a wide circle, when she felt a sudden sharp prickle of awareness, bordering almost on fright. Realised that the music was dying, and an odd silence had fallen.

Her hands stopped, and balled into sudden fists, which she buried in her lap. She turned her head to look at the courtyard's lamplit entrance, with a mixture of excitement and dread, knowing all too well as she did so exactly who would be there.

Andreas was standing in the archway, one hand negligently on his hip, the other holding a jacket slung carelessly over one shoulder. His eyes were fixed on her, a faint smile playing about his mouth. He was wearing close-fitting black trousers, and an immaculate white shirt, with the cuffs turned back to reveal tanned forearms. He was seriously clean-shaven tonight, and the thick, curling dark hair was brushed back from his face. Zoe could see at his throat the gleam of a heavy gold chain.

He looked, she thought, with a swift inward shiver, quite incredible.

As her gaze met his he inclined his head briefly and gravely in silent acknowledgement.

Zoe felt the breath catch starkly in her throat. She thought, When he comes over—what am I going to say— what am I going to do?

Then watched, astonished, as he turned away and walked to a table on the other side of the courtyard. Its occupants rose to receive him, offering an uproarious welcome, and, Zoe saw, several pretty girls were already jockeying for position.

Her heart felt suddenly like a stone in her chest. She thought blankly, Well—that's that, then.

She didn't have to worry about what to say, because he didn't want to hear it.

But what else could she have expected? He'd probably spent everything he possessed on that lunch, and then watched her walk out on him. Little wonder he was seeking more congenial company.

And that meant she was free. Which was exactly what she wanted. Well—wasn't it? So, she'd done exactly the right thing.

She picked up her wineglass and took a hasty gulp, angrily aware that a war between her rational self and some dreaming, emotional creature that she'd barely known existed had suddenly begun raging inside her, and for no good reason.

I must have a crush on him, she thought. And at my age, too. The kind of thing I never bothered with when I was a schoolgirl. Oh, God, sad or what?

And, of course, she couldn't simply get up and walk out, because that would look as if his actions had the power to hurt her. As if it mattered that he hadn't sought her. No, she would have to sit for at least another half-hour, if no more, and tough it out.

Or even more than that, she told herself wretchedly. She would have to look as if she was really enjoying the music and supremely indifferent to his presence at the same time. Rather like crossing a tightrope above a pit full of wolves. Especially when all she really wanted to do was go up to her room, bury her face in the pillow, and put her fingers in her ears. And pretend that this ache inside her did not exist.

She shivered, and drank some more wine. She didn't want to look across at him, but found her eyes straying in that direction just the same. He was bending his head, listening to the girl triumphantly occupying the seat next to him, a sloe-eyed creature with a sulky, sexy mouth, now all smiles and chatter.

Her hand was on his sleeve, Zoe noted, and her head was practically on his shoulder. No expertise needed to read that body language. In fact, the lady might as well be wearing a sign round her neck, saying 'Take me—I'm yours.' Except that he'd probably already done so on a number of occasions, she thought, biting her lip.

She was thankful when the folk dancers returned, and provided an alternative focus for her rapt attention.

But her small carafe of wine was almost empty, and there was a limit on how long she could sit, looking bright and fascinated, and anywhere but at him.

Yet she must have been doing it well, because this time she had no inkling of his approach until his voice said softly in her ear, 'Dance with me.'

She jumped, her hand catching the wineglass and sending the last remaining drops cascading across the cloth.

'Look what you've made me do.' She sounded more breathless than cross.

'I think you will be forgiven. Now, come.'

She rose, but hung back. 'I don't know any of the steps.'

'Then I shall teach you.' He walked behind her, close

but not touching, to the space that had been cleared for dancing. Evasion was impossible. She could feel the stares trained on her like searchlights from around the room, and heat invaded her face. Glimpsed Sherry looking as if she'd been poleaxed.

She whispered urgently, 'Andreas—I can't…'

'Yes,' he said quietly. 'Zoe *mou*, you can.' He produced a snowy handkerchief from his pocket, and shook it out, offering her a corner to hold. 'You see?' His smile was ironic. 'We do not even have to touch.' He paused. 'Now, there is a pattern of steps to be repeated. Watch what Soula does, and follow.'

Zoe obeyed mutely, staring down at the other girl's feet in their white stockings and flat-heeled black shoes. Stumbling a little at first, she began to copy what she was doing, listening to the insistent beat of the music—so much steadier than the thudding of her own heart—and gradually relaxing into it. Laughing as she found herself twirled one way, and then another. Gasping as the lead male dancer leapt high into the air before performing a series of amazing high kicks and even somersaults.

But, all the time, conscious of the man beside her holding the other end of the handkerchief. Joined to her, yet at a distance.

She was almost sorry when the music ended and the smiling, breathless line dispersed.

Somehow, she found herself back at her table. The stained cloth had already been cleared, she saw incredulously, and more wine had appeared, with clean glasses, and tiny cups of thick black coffee, very strong and sweet. And Andreas was sitting beside her. As, she thought shakily, he'd undoubtedly planned all along…

'So, *matia mou*,' he said softly. 'You have been lying to me.'

'Lying?' Her heart skipped a beat. He knew, she thought, who she was, and why she had come to Thania. And she wasn't prepared for this kind of confrontation—at least, not with him. 'I—I don't understand.'

'You told me you could not dance.'

'Oh,' she said. 'Oh—that.'

'Yes—*that*.' There was a note of faint mockery in his voice. 'What else could it be?' He paused. 'A little more practice, and you will be perfect.'

At dancing, she wondered, or lying?

She tried for a cool note. 'Is it necessary that I should be?'

'Why, yes,' he said. 'If you still plan to live at the Villa Danae. Or have you had second thoughts, perhaps?'

She shrugged. 'It will all depend on how negotiations go with your employer.' She paused. 'Tell me about him—this Steve Dragos.'

He drank some coffee, his expression meditative. 'What do you wish to know?'

She hesitated. 'Well—how old is he, for one thing?' *And did he ever know a girl called Gina who came here once, for another?*

'He is no longer young,' Andreas said. He gave a soft laugh. 'Although he would not thank me for saying so. And he is still of an age to be susceptible to a smile from a beautiful girl, if that is what you want to know,' he added drily.

Zoe flushed. 'It's not what I meant at all,' she disclaimed hastily. 'You—you seem very fond of him.'

It was his turn to shrug. 'He has been good to me over the years—in his way.'

'So he's bought your loyalty.' And for a lot of money, she thought. Because as well as the beautifully worked gold chain at his throat, he was wearing a watch that looked like a Rolex, except that it couldn't be. More likely, she told herself, it was one of those cheap imitations—wasn't it?

Andreas had straightened, the dark eyes sparking at her, his mouth suddenly hardening into coldness. 'You think, perhaps, that I am for sale?' His tone was quiet—dangerous. 'Then, you are quite wrong. I belong to no one but myself.'

Zoe lifted her chin. 'You take his money,' she pointed out.

'I earn what I am paid,' he said softly. 'Do not doubt it, Zoe *mou*.'

'And is scaring people witless one of your duties?' she asked baldly.

For a moment his brows snapped together, then his face relaxed into a grin. 'Who am I supposed to have frightened?' he asked lightly. 'You, *pedhi mou*? Surely not.'

'I saw the effect you had on those stupid boys today,' she said. 'And when you walked in tonight, everyone—stopped.'

'Did they, *matia mou*?' he said, with a touch of mockery. 'I did not notice. I could see only you.'

She swallowed. 'That—is so not true.'

'Yet here I am,' he said. 'With you, and no other.'

'Why?' Her breathing had quickened uncontrollably. 'Because I walked away from you today, and you needed to re-establish your ascendancy? In case word got round and you—lost face?'

He gave her a long, steady look, making her meet his gaze. 'Is that truly what you think, Zoe *mou*—that I have something to prove?'

She bit her lip. 'No,' she admitted reluctantly, at last. 'No, I don't. But I still don't understand why people seem so in awe of you.'

He was still watching her, his expression unreadable. 'Perhaps I simply benefit from the respect they give my employer.'

'Is he really so powerful—even from a distance?'

'You must judge that for yourself, *pedhi mou*, when you meet him.'

'Yes,' Zoe said without enthusiasm. 'I suppose so.' She glanced at him under her lashes. 'Do you know yet when that will be?'

'As soon as his doctors permit.' He was silent for a moment. 'If you are so impatient, *matia mou*, maybe I should introduce you to my friend Dimitrios. He deals in real estate, and could find you another property which would suit you just as well.'

'Oh, no,' Zoe said too quickly, and his brows drew together.

'You mean it must be the Villa Danae, or nothing? Why?'

She was on dangerous ground, but she managed to summon up a careless smile. 'Oh, we have a saying in the UK about property buying—location, location, location. And the Villa Danae is just perfect in that respect. I would never find anywhere that measured up to it.'

She paused. 'And it's never been lived in—allowed to achieve its full potential. I find that—tragic.'

'Ah,' he said softly. 'But even a paradise like Thania can have its share of tragedies, Zoe *mou*. And perhaps it is unwise to fix your heart on this particular house. My—boss has agreed to see you, nothing more.'

For a moment, she was tempted to confide in him—to tell him why she had come to Thania and ask for his help.

Then common sense reasserted itself, telling her to do no such stupid thing. Andreas was Steve Dragos' man. He'd made that perfectly clear. So, was it likely that he'd get involved in anything that might be contrary to the interests of such a powerful employer?

He'd get in touch with him immediately, she thought. Warn him. Because the potential loss of such an expensive and beautiful house was bound to matter.

Whatever might have happened in the past—whatever promises could have been made, time had moved on, and there was no guarantee that Mr Dragos would let Villa Danae go without a struggle.

And, no matter how many legal-sounding documents she could produce, he'd be able to hire any number of high-powered international lawyers to range against her.

Besides, instinct told her that any help she might acquire from Andreas Stephanos might well cost her more than she could afford to give.

It was better by far to keep her own counsel, she thought, swallowing, and catch Steve Dragos off guard. If that was possible.

She smiled at him, drank some wine. 'Well,' she said. 'I'll just have to keep my fingers crossed.'

'And if that doesn't work—if you don't get the house— you will leave?'

She hunched a shoulder. 'That's the plan.'

He leaned back in his chair, watching her through half-closed eyes. Paying lingering attention, she realised, to her blonde hair, piled in a loose knot on top of her head. To the low neckline of the black dress and the way it skimmed the top of her breasts. Dwelling meditatively on her mouth.

Making her know simply by a glance what it would be like to be touched—to be kissed by him, she thought in shaken bewilderment.

He smiled, as if he was perfectly aware what was on her mind.

'Then I shall have to find some way to persuade you to change your mind, *agapi mou*,' he drawled.

'Ah,' she said, snatching at her control. 'But perhaps I'm like you.'

'Like me?' He frowned slightly.

'You said you belonged to no-one,' she reminded him coolly. 'Well, neither do I. And I do just as I please.'

'But there may come a time,' he suggested softly, 'when you may also wish to—please me.'

There was a swift, taut silence, then Zoe shrugged. 'It seems to me that there are quite enough people doing that already,' she told him lightly. She managed, somehow, not to glance at the table across the room, and the sullen looks being directed at them by the Greek beauty.

His mouth twisted in wry acknowledgement. 'Maybe you have been sent to Thania to teach me the error of my ways.'

'I think that would take far more time than I have to spare,' she dismissed.

'And I think you are right, *agapi mou*.' He grinned lazily at her. 'It would probably take a lifetime. And in the meantime, I shall teach you to dance. A much easier thing.' He got to his feet. 'Come.'

Well, it was one thing she could agree to, Zoe thought with an inward sigh as she rose and followed him. Probably the only thing. And she sighed again.

It was an unforgettable evening, a breathless, exhilarating whirl of sound and rhythm, allowing her no time to think, or question the wisdom of her actions. Her head was spinning. She felt as if she were flying.

And Andreas was at her side throughout, joined to her always by that square of white linen, whispering encouragement, the dark eyes intent on her flushed, happy face.

'No more,' she protested laughingly, at last, leaning against one of the wooden posts that supported the overhead vine, a hand pressed to her side.

'But the night is only just beginning.'

Zoe shook her head. 'Not for me,' she said. 'I need to get some rest. As it is, I probably shan't be able to walk in the morning. My feet will be too sore.'

'Then ride instead.' His voice was quiet, but insistent. 'I will bring the Jeep to the hotel at ten o' clock, and show you my island.'

Zoe hesitated. Dancing with him, surrounded by a crowd of other people, was one thing. Spending a whole day together on their own was a different matter entirely.

Her throat tightened. She said, uncertainly, 'Andreas…'

'Zoe *mou*,' he returned softly. He studied her for a moment. 'Are you truly so scared to be alone with me?'

'No,' she said. 'Of course not.'

He grinned at her. 'Little liar.' He paused, his face becoming serious again. 'But I swear you have nothing to fear. You honour me with your company, nothing more.'

He added softly, 'Besides, I shall never ask anything of you, *agapi mou*, that you do not wish to give.' He put one hand under her chin, tilting up her face, making her look at him. 'Now will you come with me?'

She heard herself say, 'Why not?' And could immediately think of a thousand sane and sensible reasons to refuse. But she'd committed herself now, and she would not go back on her word. Her pride would not allow it.

She felt his thumb stroke the line of her jaw, gentle as a feather from the breast of a dove, and smothered an instinctive gasp as she felt her nipples harden instinctively against the soft fabric of her dress.

She took a hasty step backwards, jerking her chin away, and the abrupt movement proved the last straw for her already dishevelled hair, which came tumbling down onto her shoulders.

'Damn.' She made a dive for the clasp which had fallen to the floor, but Andreas was too quick for her, straightening with the worked silver clip in his hand.

'Leave it,' he advised, the dark eyes warm and slumbrous as they observed her. 'Your hair is better like that. Beautiful. And it will soon be spread across a pillow anyway,' he added softly.

Heat rose in her face. The image was too personal—too intimate, and she needed to distance herself, and fast before, dear God, that too-knowledgeable gaze of his observed her state of arousal.

She held out her hand. 'May I have my clip back, please?'

'Tomorrow,' he said, and slipped it into his trouser pocket. 'After you have seen Thania with me.'

Zoe bit her lip. She said, coldly, 'Perhaps I'll decide it isn't worth the trouble, after all.'

'Then it will stay with me,' he said, unabashed. 'A cherished memento of you, Zoe *mou*.'

'You have an answer for everything, don't you?' she said bitterly.

'Not yet,' he said. 'But I live in hope.' He allowed her to digest that, then inclined his head, coolly and courteously. '*Kalinichta, agapi mou.* Until tomorrow.'

She said in a stifled voice, 'Goodnight,' and walked away, threading her way between the tables, hardly aware any more of the curious and speculative glances coming her way.

Once in her room, she kicked off her sandals and fell, face down, across the bed, burying her face on her folded arms.

And I'm going to spend the day with him tomorrow, she groaned inwardly. I must be crazy.

She tried to comfort herself with the reflection that it would give her the opportunity to explore Thania with someone who knew the island and loved it. But it was still a high-risk situation, and she knew it.

But he promised I'd be safe, she argued with herself, defensively.

No, came the uncompromising reply. He said he'd take nothing that you didn't wish to give. That's entirely different.

And, as a guarantee, it was totally meaningless. Because he knew that she wanted him, she realised, shocked. And he was confident that, with a little time and patience, she'd be his. And of her own free will, too.

Zoe sat up slowly, pushing her hair back from her face. That's why he didn't make any move on me tonight, she told herself, bleakly. He knew I'd be expecting him to escort me to my door—to try to kiss me goodnight at the very least.

Yet he didn't. In fact, he hardly touched me.

Except once, she reminded herself, and she could still feel the marks of his fingers against her jaw as if she'd been branded there.

But during the dancing they'd always been divided by that silly handkerchief. No real physical contact at all.

This was clearly a game, she thought, for which he'd

invented his own rules a long time ago. And this worried her.

It was disturbing, too, to realise how little she still knew about him. True, it hadn't been an evening for the exchange of confidences, but he seemed to be becoming more of an enigma with every hour that passed.

But if he's a gardener, she thought, I'm Helen of Troy.

She could hear the faint sound of the music floating up to her. No doubt he'd rejoined his Greek girl, and coaxed her back to smiles by now. Maybe she'd even persuade him to spend tomorrow with her instead.

After all, they both live here, she told herself, whereas I—well, I could just be passing through.

She undressed and put on her wrap, then cleaned off the small amount of make-up she was wearing, and brushed her hair. It was thick and silky, she thought, shaking it back from her face, but it didn't make her a beauty. Nothing could, although she supposed she was on the attractive side of ordinary.

Just remember that, she told herself caustically, and take the sweet talk with a large pinch of salt.

If Andreas kept her hair clasp, she'd have to find another, she thought as she put down the brush. But there'd been a shop selling crafts and jewellery in copper and pewter as well as silver on the way up to the square. She could look there.

If Andreas didn't come tomorrow…

She was tired, she wanted to sleep, but she couldn't switch off the constant images passing and re-passing through her mind. The room felt stifling, too, and the sheets seemed to graze her like sandpaper.

Eventually, she got up, put on her wrap again, and went out onto the balcony. She sat lifting her face to the faint breeze from the harbour, listening to the lap of the sea, and the creaking of the timber caiques at anchor. There were no other sounds. The hotel lights were extinguished, and the dancers had dispersed. Andreas too would be—somewhere. Not alone, perhaps.

It shocked her to discover how much that possibility hurt. And how hard she had to fight to block the image of Andreas, his naked skin dark against the sheets of some woman's bed, his body arched above her in the act of love.

She even found herself wondering what kind of a lover he would be. Demanding or patient? Fierce or gentle? Or, maybe, all of them, she thought, and was horrified to recognise her own mounting excitement.

This was what he'd sensed, of course, from that first moment of their meeting. This was why he could take his time with her, not touching or kissing, because it would simply intensify the yearning. Make her want him more with every passing moment.

Until, inevitably, she could bear no more, and turned to him, offering herself.

Zoe shivered. It can't matter, she told herself desperately. *He* can't matter. I mustn't allow this to happen.

Yet already it seemed to be beyond her control, and she knew it.

Knew, too, that wherever Andreas had spent the night, he would be waiting for her outside the hotel in the morning, as he'd promised.

In just a few hours from now, she thought, staring blindly at the starlit sea. And I'll go with him this time—this one last time. Then, never again. Because it's too dangerous, and I can't afford to take that kind of risk.

And found, suddenly, the lonely, bitter taste of tears in her throat.

CHAPTER SIX

IT TOOK for ever next morning to decide what to wear. Zoe found herself trying and discarding almost every piece of clothing she'd brought with her.

Eventually, she picked what she would have worn had she been spending the day on her own—as, of course, she still might be, she swiftly reminded herself—putting on her blue bikini topped by a pair of white cut-off trousers, and a pretty overshirt in shades of blue and gold.

Her hair she wore deliberately pulled back from her face, and confined at the nape of her neck with a rubber band.

A glance at her watch told her it was nine-thirty, and she still had time for breakfast. Maybe food would calm the nervous churnings in her stomach, although she doubted it. But at least it would give her an occupation. Stop her prowling up and down her room, endlessly packing and repacking her canvas bag.

Sherry was quick and efficient with the rolls and coffee, but Zoe couldn't help noticing that she seemed to lack her usual ebullience.

'Hangover?' she teased as she poured herself some orange juice.

'I didn't have time to get one,' Sherry said, putting down small pots of cherry jam and honey.

'It was a terrific night,' Zoe agreed. 'But how do you stand the pace?'

'Each Sunday, I ask myself the same thing,' Sherry said wryly. She forced a shadow of her normal grin. 'Ignore me. I'm suffering from a touch of the ex-pats this morning.'

'Then you don't recommend life on Thania?'

'On the contrary, it's wonderful—with the right person,' Sherry said with bite.

'Ouch.' Zoe gave her a surprised look. 'What's Stavros done to upset you?'

'A slight difference of opinion, that's all.' Sherry paused. 'So what have you got planned for today?'

'I'm doing the island tour,' Zoe said. She hesitated. 'Actually, with Andreas—the man I was dancing with last night.'

'I noticed.' There was an odd note in Sherry's voice. 'How did you two happen to meet?'

'I told you—he's the gardener at the Villa Danae.' Zoe spread honey on a roll and took a bite. 'But judging by the way everyone jumps when he's around, I think he runs a protection racket on the side.'

Sherry's laugh rang hollow. 'Did he tell you his other name?'

'Stephanos,' Zoe said, stirring her coffee. 'Andreas Stephanos. But you must know him, surely?'

'I've seen him around, but he doesn't often come to our dance nights. I think his boss keeps him too busy.' Sherry hesitated. 'And you're seeing him today?'

'Yes.' Zoe nodded. She gave Sherry a frowning look. 'Don't you approve?'

'It's really none of my business.' There was constraint in Sherry's voice. 'Just—look after yourself, that's all.'

Zoe smiled at her. 'I intend to,' she said. 'You really don't have to worry.'

'It's just that I'm not sure if you know what you're getting into,' Sherry began, only to be halted by Stavros suddenly appearing beside her.

'Darling.' His smile did not reach his eyes. 'Some guests are asking about a packed lunch. Will you deal with it?'

Sherry bit her lip. 'Yes—I'll be right there.'

Zoe watched them go, surprised. Their usual cheerful, jokey relationship was clearly suffering from a bump in the road this morning. And when she walked through the re-

ception area a little later, she could hear the sound of a
low-voiced but furious argument coming from the office.

Zoe grimaced inwardly. She'd got to like them both, and,
whatever the problem, she hoped it would blow over soon.

Then she saw that the Jeep was parked right in front of
the hotel, and Andreas was lounging at the wheel, lean and
casual in denim shorts and a short-sleeved blue cotton shirt,
his eyes masked by sunglasses, and all other considerations
were swept from her mind.

He raised a hand in greeting as she halted uncertainly at
the top of the steps, and leapt out to take her shoulder bag
and open the passenger door for her.

'*Kalimera,*' he greeted her. 'Did you sleep well?'

'Not really.' Pointless trying to pretend the shadows under her eyes didn't exist. 'It was so hot. There seemed to
be no air.' *And there was the thought of you, burning in
my brain, refusing to let go.*

He frowned swiftly. 'I will tell Stavros to have a fan
taken to your room.'

'Oh,' Zoe said as the Jeep started off. 'Is Stavros under
your thumb, too? That could explain something.'

He shot her a sideways look as the Jeep swung up the
hill towards the square. 'What might it explain?'

Zoe looked coolly back at him. 'I don't think Sherry, his
wife, approves of me spending too much time with you,
and I'm awfully afraid they've been having a row about it.'

'I am sorry to hear it.' His tone was dry. 'But marital
quarrels are part of life, and no doubt they will enjoy the
eventual reconciliation.' He paused. 'Did Stavros' wife indicate a reason for her disapproval?'

'Not as such. She probably thinks you've acted as island
guide for too many other women tourists.'

'Then she is wrong.' There was a faint snap in his tone.
'You are the first, Zoe *mou*.'

'Well, please don't be cross about it.' Zoe suddenly realised she'd said too much and could have bitten off her
tongue. Andreas, she thought, alarmed, would be formida-

ble if angered. 'I think she was just—anxious about me,'
she added in an effort to smooth things over.

His smile was wintry. 'A concern I share with her, *pedhi
mou*. So she need have no fears. You are safe in my care.'

The Jeep turned into the square, and slowed to allow a
small boy leading a puppy on a long piece of string to cross
in front of it.

Andreas turned to look at her, his face softening. He said,
'You believe that, don't you, *agapi mou*?'

'Yes.' Zoe swallowed. 'Yes, I—I do.' And it was true,
she thought, although she could not explain her own certainty. On the other hand, perhaps she was just being ap-
pallingly naive, and would live to regret it.

He took her hand and carried it swiftly to his lips. 'Then
our day begins here,' he told her softly.

She could feel herself blushing, and glanced hurriedly
round the square instead. The backgammon players were
out in force already, she noticed with amusement.

And among them Uncle Stavros, on his feet, staring at
her and then at her companion, eyes fixed, mouth parted in
shock as if he'd seen a ghost.

Zoe tensed, feeling the force of his gaze like a slap across
the face. And as the Jeep moved off again she saw him
take a step forward, his stick raised, his face distorted by
a thunderous frown.

'Is something wrong?' Andreas was alerted by her sudden intake of breath.

'No, not a thing.' She was making no more trouble for
Stavros' family. But, all the same, what the hell was the
matter with everyone today? she asked herself in bewilderment.

She hurried into speech, trying to regain her equilibrium,
which had been jolted by the nasty little incident. 'The
church is beautiful, isn't it? I visited it yesterday.'

He grinned at her. 'Did you see the icon of the Virgin
of the Cave?'

She looked back at him, demurely. 'Not after Sherry had warned me about it.'

'I doubt that the icon by itself could do much,' Andreas returned pensively. 'Although, naturally, I have never tested its powers,' he added silkily.

'Of course not.' Zoe tried to keep a straight face, and failed abysmally.

'That's better,' he approved as she began to shake with laughter. 'Sometimes you seem to have all the cares of the world on your shoulders, *pedhi mou.*'

'Perhaps I'm just not used to having holidays.' *Or meeting someone like you.*

'Then I shall do my best to make this one special for you,' Andreas told her quietly. He paused. 'I am glad to see you are wearing shoes you can walk in. I thought we would go first to Mount Edira before it becomes too hot.'

Zoe thought privately that it was pretty warm already, but she said nothing.

The Jeep sped on. Livassi was far behind them now, and they were climbing on a road little better than a cart-track, which wound its way upwards through groves of olive trees, their silver leaves glittering in the sun. Craning her neck, Zoe could see nets spread on the ground beneath, waiting to catch the coming harvest.

'I can see the road-surfacing scheme has been a great success,' she commented breathlessly, nearly jolted out of her seat by one pothole.

'Most of the traffic has four legs,' Andreas returned. 'They manage just fine.'

The track became steeper and the olives yielded to pine trees. The air was cooler here in their shade and faintly scented with resin. Zoe sniffed pleasurably, then took it deep into her lungs.

Andreas swung the Jeep off the track, and parked on a rare level stretch under the trees.

'From here, we walk,' he said. He gave her a wry grin. 'If you are not too bruised.'

She said lightly, 'I'm tougher than I look. Lead the way.

She had half expected him to take her hand, but he did not, and in places it was something of a scramble to follow his long, sure stride. But when they reached the small concrete viewing platform that had been constructed near the summit, allowing an all-round view, she forgot everything else, drawing a breath of sheer wonder.

Her voice shook a little. 'Oh, God, it's just—so beautiful.'

'Yes,' he said. 'Each time I come here, I cannot believe that I spend time anywhere else.'

Below them was the green of the island itself, dotted with a patchwork of tiny coloured roofs, edged by faint strips of silvery sand. And beyond was the sea, stretching to the misty horizon in shades of turquoise and azure, broken only by the craggy amethyst shapes of the neighbouring islands.

'There is Zakynthos.' Andreas pointed. 'And that is Kefalonia.'

'They look almost close enough to touch.' Zoe shook her head.

'I advise a more conventional approach,' he said lazily. 'We could sail there one day, if you would like.' When she did not reply immediately, he went on smoothly, 'And the tiny one near Kefalonia is Ithaca, the place that Odysseus struggled to return to for so many years.'

'Hmm.' Zoe wrinkled her nose consideringly. 'According to the version I read, he didn't struggle that hard. In fact, he was constantly allowing himself to be diverted— generally by beautiful girls.'

Andreas tutted in amused reproof. 'Also by monsters, storms, and the malice of the old gods, Zoe *mou*. And his wife waited for him, faithfully and patiently through many long years, so he cannot have been all bad if he could inspire such devotion.

'Besides, not all the women he met were well disposed towards him,' he added. 'After all, Circe turned his men into animals.'

Zoe gave him a limpid look. 'Someone once suggested that Circe was the first feminist.'

'*Po, po, po,*' he said softly. 'And do you share her view, *agapi mou*, and believe that all men are beasts?'

'No, of course not.' She hesitated. 'Although the pair I encountered yesterday made me wonder.'

'They have spent too much time away from Thania,' he said, with faint contempt. 'Working in bars and clubs where foreign girls get drunk, and strip off their clothes, and encourage men to do the same. So, to their limited reason, all foreign girls must be like that. But that is not an excuse,' he added levelly.

'No,' Zoe said. She paused awkwardly. 'Andreas—I didn't thank you properly yesterday for rescuing me, and I want to apologise for that.'

'It's not a problem.' He shrugged. 'You were upset.' He pointed again. 'Do you see that little bay? That is where legend says Odysseus rested before the gods allowed him to return at last to his home. I thought maybe we could swim there this afternoon. That is, of course, if you have brought your swimming costume.'

'And if I haven't?'

He smiled at her. 'Then we shall still swim, *matia mou*,' he said softly. 'But I shall keep my eyes closed.' He paused. 'However, I would bet good money that it will not be necessary. That you are wearing a bikini under those charming clothes.'

Zoe bit her quivering lip. 'You see altogether too much, Mr Stephanos.'

He shrugged again. 'Perhaps because I like to look. And to look at you, Zoe *mou*, is a pleasure.' His smile widened. 'And what of you?' he questioned gently. 'Have you seen enough?'

If he meant himself, Zoe thought with a pang, then she would never see enough. She could go on filling her eyes with him for the rest of her life. Not a realisation to give her much pleasure or peace of mind.

Hurriedly, she swung round, shading her eyes. 'Can we see the Villa Danae from here?'

'Yes, if you have the eyes of a hawk.' His hands descended on her shoulders, turning her slightly, forcing her to control an involuntary quiver of response. 'There is the beach, and that little spot of colour is the roof. You see?'

Zoe peered down. 'And your own home—where is that?'

His brows lifted. 'Are you planning to pay me a visit?'

'No,' she denied quickly. 'Just—curious.'

'It is not easy to distinguish from this height,' Andreas said after a pause. 'The roof tiles are green and a little faded. But one day, soon, I will show you—if you wish.'

She said haltingly, 'Well—perhaps.' Then, 'Shall we go down, now?'

If the climb up had been something of a struggle, the descent was even more difficult. Even in her flat canvas shoes, Zoe found she was constantly slipping on the loose earth and pine needles.

And once she lost her footing altogether and cried out as she began to slide downhill. Andreas, walking ahead, immediately spun round and grabbed her, holding her against him to steady her. And for a few heart-stopping seconds she felt the strength of him, and the heat penetrating her thin layer of clothing as if it did not exist. She was aware of his breath on her face, drank in the warm scent of his skin with shaking voracity. As his clasp tightened she thought, He's going to kiss me, and her whole body tingled with longing and delight.

Then, with abrupt suddenness, she was free. Set at a brief but definite distance. She could have wept with the disappointment of it. And with the shock of what, she realised, was a rejection.

Her face burned, and she could not meet his gaze. 'I'm sorry,' she mumbled. 'That was clumsy of me.'

'No, *agapi mou*,' he said. 'The fault is mine. After all, I promised to take care of you.'

He took her hand firmly in his for the rest of the way,

helping her over the steepest sections of the track. But if he'd been a paid guide, his touch could hardly have been more impersonal.

By the time they got back to the Jeep, Zoe's heart was thumping like a trip-hammer, but it had nothing to do with the gradient. Because she knew that her feelings and desires back there on the mountain must have been shamingly transparent. He could not have missed the blatant signals she'd been giving out as her body had been pressed to his. So, why had he chosen to ignore them?

He knew I wanted him, she thought, humiliated. He must have known. I did everything but put my arms round his neck and draw him down to me.

I shall never ask anything of you, agapi mou, *that you do not wish to give*. His own words, still teasing at her mind—even stinging a little.

But she had wanted to give, she thought wretchedly. She'd needed his arms to hold her, and his mouth to find hers, and he had turned away—kindly, courteously, but definitely.

Because, presumably, he was regretting his pursuit of her. He was tired of the game he'd been playing, and decided to end it.

And now, somehow, she had to deal with her own regrets.

'Are you all right, *pedhi mou*?' He had shut the passenger door of the Jeep, and was regarding her with a faint frown.

Make it mundane, she thought. Bring the situation back to basics, as if a few moments ago had never happened.

'I'm a little thirsty,' she admitted, sounding half amused, half apologetic. 'Because things were a bit fraught at the hotel, I forgot to bring any water.'

'I have some in a cool-bag,' he said. He paused. 'But I also have a better idea, if you can wait for a minute or two.'

'Whatever you say.' She achieved a smile. Kept it cool and friendly. 'You're in charge, after all.'

She'd expected to be driven to a village with a *kafeneion*, but at the foot of the track he turned the Jeep onto a path between the olive trees until they came to a small, single-storey house, painted white, and almost fiercely neat in spite of the chickens pecking in the dust outside the only door.

A small woman emerged from the house, dressed in black, her hair covered by a scarf, her broad smile revealing gaps in her teeth. As Andreas climbed out of the Jeep to greet her she burst into a flood of shrill Greek, reaching up to pat him on the shoulder.

Then she snatched up a pitcher like a flower vase from a rickety table outside the door, and trotted off round the house with it.

'Come down, *agapi mou*, and meet Androula,' Andreas invited, walking round to the passenger side. 'She is an old friend, and she has gone to fetch us some water from her own spring, which comes straight from the mountain—the nearest we have to nectar.'

Zoe got out of the Jeep. 'Are you sure about this?' She glanced around her. 'Certain we're not imposing on her?'

'She loves company,' he said. 'And she will be delighted that I have brought you to her.'

'Does she live alone here?' Zoe asked doubtfully. 'It's very isolated.'

'No, she lives with Spiros, her husband, but he will be off attending to his melon patch.'

Androula was back, almost at once, her pitcher brimming. Nodding and smiling, she offered it to Zoe first.

The water was crystal clear, and so cold that it made her gasp. Zoe drank deeply, thirstily relishing its chill against the burn of her throat.

'Good?' Andreas asked as she lowered the pitcher at last.

'Better than that.'

To her surprise, he took the pitcher from her, and drank

in turn while Androula smiled widely, nodding her approval.

Zoe wasn't sure how she felt about it. In a way, sharing the container was almost as intimate as a kiss. But perhaps Androula was simply short of glasses, she told herself. And, anyway, it was no big deal. She could not allow it to be.

Androula put a small brown hand on her arm, gesturing towards the house with the other.

'She wishes you to go in, and sample her honey cakes,' Andreas explained. 'A mark of great favour,' he added.

She said lightly, 'Then how can I resist?'

Inside, the house seemed to consist of one spotlessly clean room. Curtained alcoves built into the thick walls contained beds, and there was also a fireplace, a stove for cooking, a table and some hard-looking chairs. On the top of a chest of drawers was an icon of the Virgin and Child, with a votive light burning beside it.

One wall lit up the rest of the rather gloomy interior, covered as it was from top to bottom in vivid picture postcards from every corner of the world.

'From their son,' Andreas said, seeing her looking at them, while Androula bustled around. 'He was a merchant seaman, and travelled everywhere. And, unlike Odysseus, always he sent cards home so that they would know where he was, and that he was safe.'

'And is he still safe?'

'Very much so,' Andreas said drily. 'He met an Australian girl, and now he lives in Queensland. Every six months he sends his parents the money for their airfares, so that they can visit him, and they put it in the bank instead, so it will be there for him if disaster should strike.'

'What a shame,' Zoe said softly. 'Do you think they will ever go?'

'I doubt it. I think he will have to bring his wife and child to them instead. And then, of course, he will stay. Or so Androula believes.'

'She thinks he'll give up the good life in Australia for Thania? Why?'

'Because of the water from the spring,' he said after a pause. 'There is an old superstition that anyone who drinks it will always return here.'

In the deafening silence that followed, Zoe heard herself swallow. She said huskily, 'Then it's a good thing I'm not superstitious.'

Andreas smiled at her. 'And neither am I, *matia mou*,' he said softly. 'Neither am I.'

The honey cakes were delicious and Zoe could praise them without reserve, while Andreas translated for her.

When it was time to leave, Zoe found her hands clasped between Androula's gnarled ones, while the older woman spoke to her softly and earnestly.

'What did she say?' Zoe asked as they emerged into the sunlight. 'I feel such an idiot not to be able to understand.'

His voice was expressionless. 'That she will pray to the Virgin of the Cave to send you tall sons.'

She kept her smile in place as if it had been nailed there. 'Wonderful,' she said, lightly. 'My entire future mapped out on the strength of one drink of water. Maybe I should stick to the bottled Loutraki brand from now on.'

Andreas made no reply, simply revved the engine and started off, sending dust and pebbles flying.

Back on the road, they travelled a mile, perhaps two, in a silence that Zoe was the first to break. 'Are we going to Odysseus' bay?'

'It's on the other side of the island.' He didn't look at her. 'I thought we would have lunch first. I know a good place.'

'Run by another friend of yours?'

His wintry expression eased a little. 'No one can have too many friends, *pedhi mou*.'

'No,' she said quietly. 'I'm sure that's true.'

She'd had friends, she thought, at school and later at university, but over the last few traumatic years, when Gina had been her priority, she'd lost touch with most of them. That was something she would start to rectify as soon as she got home. She might even use one of the internet sites that reunited people. It would all be part of her fresh start—her new life. Once she had laid the ghosts of the past...

'You are sighing,' Andreas said. 'What makes you sad?'

'I didn't realise I was.' Zoe hesitated. 'Perhaps all this wonderful sun and scenery reminded me that this is only a holiday, and that there's a long winter ahead at home.'

'But winter also has its pleasures, Zoe *mou*,' he said. 'If you have the right person to share them with.'

But I shan't have you... Her hands gripped together, white-knuckled, at the sudden pain of it.

Oh, dear God, she thought. How can I be feeling like this? I never meant it to happen.

Was this how her mother had felt all those years ago? she asked herself with a kind of desperation. And was this why she had never returned—never accepted possession of the house that had been given to her? Because she was suddenly overwhelmed—terrified by the force of her own emotions?

And so she'd opted instead for safety—security in England, with only the picture she'd painted to remind her of what she'd left behind.

And I, she thought, I shall only have a few photographs.

She was aware of Andreas' swift, sidelong glance, and hurried into speech. 'I've just realised I forgot to take my camera up Mount Edira. How stupid of me. I could have got some marvellous shots.'

'Another time, maybe,' he said. 'When perhaps you will trust me enough, *pedhi mou*, to tell me what you are really thinking.'

To which, Zoe decided in confusion, there was really no answer. Or not one that she dared to give.

They had the Bay of Odysseus all to themselves.

Zoe's brows lifted as she surveyed the deserted crescent

of sand. 'Did you arrange for everyone else to stay away?' she asked, not altogether joking.

Andreas smiled at her, unfazed. 'People usually come here by boat,' he explained. 'To swim and to dive. But there are no trips on Sundays.' He paused. 'As you must have noticed, it is not particularly accessible unless you have a four-wheel drive.'

'And not even then,' Zoe said, wincing at the memory of the bone-jolting ride through olive groves and citrus orchards, ending in the descent of a track like an Alpine black run.

'Also, it is not seen as a family beach,' he added. 'It shelves very deeply and quickly about fifty yards out, and, if you are not a strong swimmer, you are soon out of your depth.'

His warning came too late, Zoe thought, suppressing a bubble of hysteria. She'd been out of her depth since the moment she'd set eyes on him. And agreeing to spend the day with him—accompanying him to this silent and solitary place—was madness.

She said quietly, 'Then I shall have to be careful.' She paused. 'But if it's dangerous, why would anyone come here?' She glanced around. 'And there are certainly no concessions for tourists,' she added wryly.

'They come for the legend.' Andreas pointed to a large flat rock, gleaming white in the sun, jutting out into the sea at one end of the cove. 'They like to dive from the place where Odysseus is supposed to have rested before beginning the final leg of his journey to Ithaca.'

'You sound sceptical.'

He shrugged. 'He was on board a friendly ship, with a fair wind. Why hesitate when Ithaca was within reach?'

She looked down at the rough ground. 'Maybe he encountered yet another willing nymph.' Her voice sounded almost stifled.

'The story does not mention one.'

She swallowed. 'Then perhaps, after all those setbacks,

he was simply scared of being happy again with the people he loved. Petrified that something else would go wrong. And he decided he needed a breathing space.' She paused. 'I suppose you would have sailed straight on.'

'When what you want most in the world is within reach,' he said softly, 'why hold back?'

He went back to the Jeep, and began to unpack the rug, the sun umbrella and the cool-bag from the back, leaving her to stare after him, her heart thumping against her ribs in mingled excitement and unease.

She turned and began to walk down the beach, feeling the burn of the sand through the soles of her canvas shoes.

It was bakingly hot, the sea still and almost colourless, the horizon a distant shimmer.

She had not expected to be alone with him here, she thought. It might be off the beaten track, but it was justly a famous beauty spot. Besides, the taverna, where they'd eaten a wonderful lunch of freshly grilled fish and salad, had been equally remote, clinging to the edge of a cliff, but almost every table had been occupied.

She lifted a hand, pushing a strand of sweat-dampened hair from her forehead, recalling the boisterous welcome they'd received from Takis, the owner, a large, bearded man with a booming laugh. He'd clapped Andreas cheerfully on the shoulder as he'd shown them to their table, and subjected Zoe to a long look that had combined frank appreciation with curiosity.

But when he'd made some jovial comment in his own language, he'd encountered a frosty glance from Andreas that had sent him speeding back to his charcoal grill.

And when she'd enquired what Takis had said to provoke such a reaction, Andreas had returned coolly and dismissively that it was unimportant, and asked her if she would like some wine.

Clearly one was allowed to trespass so far and no further, she thought. And maybe she should remember that.

When she turned back the sun umbrella was in place, the

rug was spread beneath it, and Andreas was stripping off his outer clothing to reveal brief swimming trunks.

She halted, feeling her mouth go dry. It was easier, she thought, struggling for detachment, not to look at him.

He went past her, running with lithe grace, and plunged into the sea, his body cutting the water like a knife, with scarcely a splash.

Last time, of course, this had been her signal to leave, but today there was nowhere to run. They were isolated and alone together.

Yet so we were on Mount Edira, she reminded herself, and he didn't touch me.

But that was then, she thought as she began to unbutton her shirt. And this is now... And what am I most scared of, anyway: that he'll lay a hand on me—or that he won't?

When he returned she was stretched out in the shadow of the umbrella, sunblock applied, her hair tucked into her white cotton hat, sunglasses in place, and her attention apparently concentrated on the book she was reading. Even if her whole body was tingling in awareness of him, she appeared cool, and that was what mattered.

He picked up his towel, and began to blot the moisture from his skin. She knew that he was looking down at her, the dark eyes travelling slowly over her body. 'Are you going to swim, Zoe *mou*?'

'Later, perhaps.' She kept her tone light. 'I tend to keep out of deep water.'

There was a smile in his voice. 'And you are never tempted to throw caution to the winds?'

'Rarely.' The words on the page danced in front of her in a meaningless jumble. 'I like to keep life simple—and safe.'

'I too prefer to avoid complications,' he said. 'But sometimes they are inevitable.'

He stretched out beside her, close but not touching. Very much at his ease.

He said softly, 'I am sure that is a fascinating book, *pedhi mou*, but I would be grateful if you could put it down. Because we need to talk, you and I.'

Zoe hesitated, then complied reluctantly. She said, 'What do you want to talk about?'

'About you, *matia mou*—what else?'

Her laugh cracked in the middle. 'Not a very interesting subject.'

'Ah,' he said. 'But I disagree. You see, Zoe *mou*, you intrigue me. So, I wish to know exactly what brought you here to Thania. And this time I want the truth.'

CHAPTER SEVEN

ZOE sat bolt upright, and stared at Andreas. He was lying propped up on one elbow, very much at his ease, the dark eyes slightly narrowed, the firm mouth cool and unsmiling, as he looked back at her.

The silence seemed to echo between them. The whisper of the sea only a few yards away seemed suddenly like muted thunder to her heightened senses. Her skin tingled under his unwavering gaze.

He said, 'I am waiting for you to answer, *pedhi mou*.'

She swallowed. 'I—I don't know what you're talking about.'

'You disappoint me.'

She spread her hands defensively. 'I came here on holiday. So do a lot of other people.'

'Not that many,' he said. 'Compared with other islands. And they come in couples, or family groups.' He paused. 'There are few beautiful girls travelling alone.' His faint smile did not reach his eyes. 'So, you must see you are something of an enigma, Zoe *mou*.'

'I don't see why.' She lifted her chin. 'It was a spur of the moment booking. My friends had already made their travel plans. And I—I needed a break. I told you why.'

'Yes,' he said. 'You have known great sadness, and I am sorry. All the more reason, I would have thought, to seek company.'

'I'll try and remember that,' she said. 'Next time.'

'But I ask again,' he went on. 'Why this island of all others? And what brought you to the Villa Danae? You understand why I am intrigued.'

'No,' she said. 'I don't.' She touched the tip of her

104

tongue to her dry lips. 'I'm surprised you don't set up some special immigration desk where the ferry docks. Interrogate everyone who comes here about their background and motivation. Or would that dent the Greek reputation for hospitality?'

Andreas shrugged a shoulder. 'Most of the people who come here are just looking for a quiet holiday in the sun. There is no need to question them. But from the first, Zoe *mou*, you have made me wonder. You are a mystery I have yet to solve.'

'And what about yourself?' She flung back her head, deliberately confrontational. 'You're hardly the simple man of the soil you claim to be. Not when you stride about, putting the fear of God into people, like the uncrowned king of the island,' she added hotly.

'Not quite king,' Andreas drawled. 'Heir to the throne, maybe.'

In the sudden deafening silence, Zoe heard herself swallow. She said with controlled calm, 'I—see. Then I don't suppose you're even called Andreas Stephanos—are you?'

'Those are my names,' he said softly. 'But there is another. My last name is Dragos.'

'Of course it is.' She tried to smile. To conceal the fact that anguish had settled like a stone in the pit of her stomach. 'Brother—cousin—nephew of Steve Dragos the shipping tycoon by any chance?'

His mouth tightened. 'His son.' He paused. 'And, like yourself, Zoe *mou*, an only child.'

'You mean we actually have something in common?' Her laugh cracked in the middle. 'But that's the only similarity. Nobody jumps when I walk into a place. Or ever will.'

She shook her head, almost wonderingly. 'Sherry wanted to warn me, I see that now, but her husband wouldn't allow it. After all, the young master must be allowed to have his fun.' She gave him a burning look. 'What a fool I've been.'

'Ah, no,' Andreas said quietly. 'I have never, from the

first moment we met, thought you were a fool, *pedhi mou*. But I must ask you not to treat me like one, either,' he added levelly.

'I think,' she said. 'The less I have to do with you, Mr Dragos, the better.' She reached for her shirt, angrily aware that her hands were shaking. 'I'd like to go back to my hotel, now, please.'

'Thania is only a small island,' he said musingly. 'But to walk such a distance in this heat? I don't think you would make it.'

'You mean you're not prepared to drive me back?' Her voice quivered with outrage.

'Certainly,' he said. 'But later. After we have spent some time together, Zoe *mou*, without fear of interruption. And when you have answered my questions,' he added softly. 'Because something tells me you are still not being completely honest.'

'You dare to say that?' Zoe almost choked on the words. 'After the way you pretended to be a gardener?'

'There was no pretence. I enjoy gardening. And, if you recall, I said I had other duties.' He shrugged again. 'If you had asked me, I would have described them to you.'

'Yes,' she said smoulderingly. 'Just like you told me your name—with the salient bit held back.'

'Well, perhaps.' He had the gall to grin at her. 'It was good, for once, to be with a woman who did not know who I was, and did not care. Someone who did not even wish me to pay her attention. But the game is over now.'

He sat up. Moved slightly so that he was closer. Close enough to touch, she realised, dry-mouthed.

'So, what salient bits are you holding back, *matia mou*?' he asked softly. 'What is your interest in the Villa Danae— which, you must acknowledge, you could not afford to rent or buy?'

'I—saw a picture of it once,' she said. 'A water colour, painted by an artist I—knew. A view of the terrace.' She shrugged. 'I wanted to see if the real thing matched the image.'

'I could almost ask the same of you, Zoe *mou*.'

She bit her lip. 'That's—not fair.'

'You think not?' There was a faint note of derision in his voice. 'You truly expect me to believe that a picture brought you here? I did not know such a thing existed.'

'You don't think the Villa Danae is worth painting?'

'Every island in Greece has its share of artists,' Andreas said slowly. 'But usually they try to capture the light—the colour of the sea. And most would choose an ancient temple to paint rather than a modern house.'

'So, it's a one-off,' Zoe said steadily. 'Maybe that's why it caught my imagination.'

'I would also be interested to know how this artist gained access,' he said, with a touch of grimness. 'I must tell my father that our security should be overhauled.'

'Why bother him with it? It was all a long time ago, and it won't happen again.' She encountered an ironic look, and flushed. 'Well, I certainly shan't be going back. You're right—the house is out of my league.' *And not just the house…*

There was a pain inside her like an iron fist clenching, and she drew a deep breath, 'But I hated seeing it empty, so I let myself dream for a while.' *So many dreams…*

She paused. 'Now I'm only sorry I ever went within a mile of the place,' she added in a small wintry voice. 'So can you call off the inquisition, please?'

'But if I am not allowed to ask questions, how can I learn all the things I wish to discover about you, Zoe *mou*?'

He spoke gently, with a hint of laughter in his voice. The sudden change of tack caught her completely off guard, and brought a swift warmth to her face that owed nothing to the sun. Because this was no confrontation over a house. This was simply a man and a woman alone together. A situation as old as time and as compelling.

She said, stumbling a little, 'What do you want to know?'

'Everything.' His eyes met hers. Held them. Making her aware of the smile in their dark depths. And the smoulder of heat, controlled but palpable. Somehow, he seemed to have moved even nearer, and she realised that if she did no more than turn carelessly her skin would brush his.

'Rather a crowded agenda for an afternoon on the beach.' She managed to speak lightly, in spite of the hectic plunge of her heart against her ribs.

'I learn quickly. And besides, you have all my attention, *matia mou*.'

Was that supposed to make her feel any better? Zoe wondered breathlessly. She looked away, picking up a handful of sand, and letting it drift through her fingers.

'Actually, there isn't all that much to tell. I had a very ordinary, happy childhood, did reasonably well at school, and got a decent degree afterwards.' She forced a smile. 'Pretty dull, really.'

'On the contrary, Zoe *mou*. A happy childhood is a gift from the gods.' There was an odd, almost bitter note in his voice.

She glanced at him quickly, noting the taut line of his mouth. 'You can't have lacked for much.'

'Materially, no, as you would expect,' he admitted flatly. 'But—in other ways…' He paused, then said with an effort, 'Unlike you, I saw little of my parents. My father was always busy—never in the same place for more than a few days at a time. And my mother was rarely well enough to be with me. She spent a lot of her life in hospitals and clinics, or searching for new treatments in Europe and America.'

'I'm—sorry.' Zoe hesitated. 'What was the matter with her?'

'I do not believe she was ever strong.' His tone was sombre. 'She found pregnancy an ordeal, and giving birth to me a nightmare. It was certainly a trauma that always seemed to stay with her throughout her life. She had constant problems with depression, and she suffered various physical symptoms over the years, too. Endless tests were carried out, but they always proved inconclusive.'

His mouth twisted. 'With hindsight, I suspect she was simply allergic to marriage—especially to marriage with a strong, demanding man like my father,' he added wryly. 'Someone who wanted a woman to stand at his side, and give him a whole nursery full of children.'

He sighed. 'I wonder sometimes which of them was the most unhappy.' He sent her a dry look. 'So you see, *pedhi mou*, I had everything I could want—except what I really wanted.'

Zoe stared at him, seeing not the cool, sexy man who'd imposed himself on her life with such casual assurance, but the boy he'd once been, existing in some bewildered, lonely vacuum.

She heard herself say his name. Put out a hand, and touched his bare shoulder, letting her palm linger on its smooth warmth. She felt the strong muscles tense beneath her touch, then Andreas captured her fingers with his own, and carried them to the faint roughness of his cheek, before brushing them swiftly with his lips.

She was lanced, almost torn apart with the sudden force of her need. She looked down at the lean, brown fingers clasping hers, and imagined them cupping her breasts, or gliding down to part her thighs. Discovering every sweet, intimate secret she had to offer. She thought of his mouth on hers. Their bodies locked together in mutual possession.

She felt her nipples blossom to heated peaks against the confines of her bikini top, and almost before she knew what she was doing her free hand was searching for the clip, and releasing it, allowing the tiny garment to fall away from her body, revealing the beauty of her small round breasts.

Her eyes met his in mute offering. She was burning, melting with the desire to be in his arms at last. To know the caress of his hands—his mouth.

She heard his harsh, indrawn breath as he looked at her. Saw the swift flare in the dark eyes.

Only to find, in the next instant, her hand released, and Andreas suddenly turning away—deliberately distancing himself, she realised with shock and disbelief.

'What's wrong?' Her voice was a stranger's, small and husky, stumbling over the words it was forming. 'Don't—don't you—want me?'

He said, over his shoulder, 'You are temptation itself, *pedhi mou*. But this is not the time or the place. So be good enough to cover yourself.'

For a moment, she knelt beside him, stricken, staring at the long line of his bare back. But even as she tried to make her fumbling fingers obey him, anger began to build in place of the agonised wrench of humiliation at his rejection of her.

She removed her top completely, and dropped it onto the sand in a gesture of total bravado.

'Isn't it time you joined the twenty-first century, Mr Dragos?' She managed mockery, edged with contempt. 'After all, I saw plenty of girls sunbathing topless on the town beach the other day. Don't you think your reaction is just a tad extreme?'

'The women you refer to make their own choices.' His tone bit. He did not look at her. 'They are not, however, alone with me here.'

'No,' she said. 'And how fortunate for them.' She got to her feet, grabbing her towel and bag. 'But as we seem to be stuck with each other, all I can do is remove myself from your immediate vicinity.'

She stalked off, down the beach, making for Odysseus' rock, her head held high. The slab of stone scorched the soles of her feet as she spread out her towel, but she refused to allow her discomfort to show, certain that Andreas would be watching.

Well, let him look, she thought, biting her lip. Just as long as he didn't realise she was actually dying of self-consciousness, parading around without her bra. Because topless sunbathing was something she'd never indulged in. Even with Mick, she'd been shy—reserved about nakedness, and she was beginning to regret her defiant gesture, which now seemed plain silly.

Face it, she told herself. You're not cut out to be one of Odysseus' nymphs.

And any form of sunbathing was out on this rock, anyway, she thought, biting her lip. There was no shade at all, and even with high-factor sun lotion she'd be risking getting badly burned.

'Oh, damn you, Andreas Dragos,' she whispered under her breath. 'You pushed me into this, and now I have to deal with it.'

She was also furiously aware that there were tears pricking at her eyelids. And she was not, under any circumstances, going to let him see her cry. Allow him to know that he had the power to hurt her so badly that she could have moaned with the pain of it.

There seemed little alternative but to go for a quick swim. It would cool her, and calm her down. Besides, drops of sea water would be good camouflage for any tears that managed to escape.

She trod, wincing, to the edge of the rock, steadied herself, stood poised for a moment, then dived in.

As she launched herself she thought she heard Andreas calling something to her.

But if it's an apology, it's too late, she told herself, gasping at the shock of the cool water against her overheated skin, and the endless green darkness waiting for her. Andreas had not exaggerated, it seemed. This was far, far deeper than she was accustomed to.

She turned, kicking her way back to the dazzle of sunlight above her, grateful when she broke the surface at last, gasping for air.

Without even glancing in the direction of the beach, she broke into her steady crawl, and headed off determinedly down the small bay. She would do the equivalent of a couple of lengths, she decided, then return to that gridiron of a rock, and plaster herself in sunblock.

She was a competent swimmer, but not a particularly strong one, and the Ionian Sea, she soon realised, was no small-town swimming pool. One length, not two, would be quite enough, she decided, discovering that she did not care for the sensation of knowing that, for the first time ever, she was completely out of her depth in water. Never before, and never again, she promised herself grimly as she turned to swim back.

But she soon found that getting back to the rock, or even inshore, was more of a problem than she'd anticipated. There was a definite current, quiet and insidious, which was pulling her out even deeper, and preventing her from making any real headway as she battled against it.

She was beginning to get tired, too, but there was no point in turning onto her back and floating, because that would simply add to her problems.

She could see Odysseus' rock, shining in the sunlight like a beacon, but a beacon that seemed to be getting further away, despite her best efforts. The drag of the current appeared to be getting stronger, or was it just that she herself was becoming weaker?

She swallowed a mouthful of sea water, and came up spluttering, trying to tread water, suddenly afraid.

She hadn't even realised she was no longer alone until strong hands took hold of her, and Andreas' voice said curtly, 'I have you now. Relax, don't struggle and I'll take you in.'

She wanted to tell him with dignity that she knew better than to resist when her life was being saved, but she got another mouthful of sea water and choked instead.

Besides, she thought, recovering, there was nothing remotely dignified in being towed back to land like a piece of flotsam.

'We are at the rock,' his voice told her breathlessly at

last. 'Turn yourself, and hold onto it with both hands, and I will pull you up.'

Zoe clung on, gasping, as he lifted himself lithely out of the water. Then his hands were under her armpits like steel clamps, drawing her up beside him.

She wasn't sure whether she wanted to burst into tears first, or be sick.

She said in a voice she hardly recognised, 'I don't know how to thank you…'

'Thank me?' he came back at her hoarsely. His eyes were sparking with anger, his mouth set grimly. 'Thank me, you little fool? *Otheos*, you could have drowned. Didn't you hear me shouting, telling you not to dive from the rock—that it can be dangerous?'

'I—I couldn't hear what you said.' Her teeth were chattering suddenly as the realisation of what might have happened washed over her again.

He muttered something under his breath that she was glad not to understand, and enveloped her without ceremony in her towel, which he had snatched up.

She'd wondered what his hands would feel like on her body, and now she knew, and they were not tender, or gentle or even remotely loverlike. They were harsh, vigorous, and extremely thorough, but she began to feel alive again, and less like a piece of wreckage.

And when he'd finished he picked up her bag, and slung it over one shoulder, then lifted Zoe, towel and all, into his arms, and carried her back to the shelter of the sun umbrella. Where he set her on her feet.

He handed her a bottle of water. 'Drink some of this.'

She was glad of its coolness against her burning throat. She poured some of the water into her cupped hand and splashed it on her stinging eyes.

Her bikini top was still lying where she had dropped it. She bent and retrieved it, trying to huddle into it under the concealment of the slipping towel.

He said levelly, 'Isn't it a little late for such modesty?'

He took the towel from her shoulders, and tossed it to one side, then fastened the clip of her bra himself. 'Nor was there any need to remove this,' he added quietly. 'My imagination had already told me how you would look without your clothes.'

She turned to face him, but found it was beyond her, so stared down at the sand instead.

She said in a low voice, 'I'm sorry. I—I lost my temper, and put us both in danger.'

'From now on,' he said, 'you will swim only from the beach at the villa. It is shallower there. And, then, only when I am present.'

She shook her head, wearily. 'I'd have thought I was the last person you'd want around.'

'No, *pedhi mou*.' He spoke more gently. 'You know that is not true.'

'I don't think I know anything,' she said. 'Not any more.'

She'd been so determined not to cry in front of him, but suddenly the tears were there, just the same, running down her face, dripping off her lashes and the tip of her nose. And she was powerless to prevent them.

'Ah, no,' he said, and his arms went round her, drawing her to him. 'No, there is no need for this, Zoe *mou*. We are both safe.'

He stroked the damp tangle of her hair, murmuring to her in his own language, while Zoe leaned against him, resting her cheek against the wall of his chest, absorbing the cool, fresh scent of the sea on his skin, the strong beat of his heart, as she tried to control her little, shuddering sobs.

She felt a strange kind of lassitude stealing over her, and her legs were shaking so badly that, if Andreas had not been holding her, she thought she would have slipped down to the sand at his feet. And stayed there for ever.

It's shock, she told herself. Delayed shock, that's all.

And knew that was only part of it.

She thought 'I don't understand,' and only realised she had spoken aloud when he answered her.

'What do you find puzzling, *pedhi mou*?'

'What we're doing here,' she said. She turned her head a fraction so that her mouth rested hungrily against his skin. 'Why you're even with me, when you don't—' Her voice faltered. 'When you don't seem to want me…'

His hands gripped her shoulders, putting her away from him as he looked gravely down at her, the dark eyes searching hers with strange intensity.

'Is this truly what you think?' he asked softly. 'Is this what you expect of me—a few hours of pleasure for you to giggle over with your girlfriends during that long English winter?'

'No.' Her mouth trembled. '*No*. But the truth is I don't know what to expect—or what's happening to me. And that scares me.' She took a step backwards, wrapping her arms round her body. Trying to close herself off from him. Establish some physical and emotional independence, but knowing at the same time that it was way too late for that. That she was lost.

She said, her voice breaking huskily, 'Oh God, I did not—*not*—come here for this.'

'You think I did?' He laughed harshly. 'You are wrong, Zoe *mou*. I had my life in place. I knew its rules and obligations. And you, believe me, were never part of the plan.'

Her voice was little more than a whisper. 'Then let me go—Andreas, please. Let me go—now.'

'You could do that?' He stared at her. 'You could walk away.'

Her mouth twisted in a painful travesty of a smile. 'I could—try.'

'Ah, no, *matia mou*,' he said unevenly. 'You know better than that. And never think that I do not desire you—because I do, more than you will ever know.' His voice deepened to a new intensity. 'But it would be too soon, and you must be aware of that, too. We have known each other only for hours, rather than weeks, months and years. And we need more time—if only to come to terms with what has happened to us. Time to learn about each other, and reach acceptance.'

'But we don't have that sort of time,' Zoe objected raggedly. 'I'm here on holiday, and when it's over I have to go back to England, to my flat and my work.' She shook her head wretchedly. 'However much you dress it up, it can only ever be a temporary affair.'

'Only,' he said, 'if that is what you want, Zoe *mou*. So, be truthful. Is it?'

Mutely, Zoe shook her head.

'Then there is no problem,' Andreas said. 'Because that is not my wish either. You see, I do not just want your body, *agapi mou*.' He framed her face gently in his hands. 'I need your heart, your soul, and that sweet, stubborn mind that will not allow you, even at this moment, to trust me. And no less will do.'

He smiled ruefully, 'And this is also why I dare not trust myself to touch you more than this. Because I am determined to behave well.'

Her voice shook. 'Andreas—there's something I have to tell you.' Her eyes searched his anxiously. 'There—there was someone else—once. I—I'm not a virgin.'

His brows lifted. 'You think that makes some difference?'

'Well—doesn't it?'

'Is he still important in your life?'

'God, no.' She thought for a moment, frowning a little. 'I can barely remember what he looked like.'

'Good,' he said. 'Then put him from your mind.' He stroked the curve of her cheek. 'If it is the moment for confessions, then maybe I should tell you that I am not a virgin either,' he added wryly.

She was startled into a giggle.

'That's much better,' he approved softly. 'I began to think you would never smile again.'

There would never be a better moment to be totally honest with him, and Zoe knew it. To tell him why she had come to Thania, and what had taken her to the Villa Danae.

But she was scared. Frightened in case she saw the tenderness fade from his eyes, and anger harden his mouth.

And in case he believed her acknowledged longing for him was motivated by self-interest rather than passion, now that she knew his true identity.

She thought, I couldn't bear that. I can't take the risk—not yet. Perhaps not ever.

Because, she realised with sudden, startling insight, the villa doesn't matter any more, or anything that may have happened in the past. All I care about is Andreas, and our future together, and I don't want it muddled by old mysteries. So, I can just tear up the paperwork, and be free of it all.

'Hey,' Andreas said softly. 'Where are you, Zoe *mou*? Suddenly, you've gone from me.'

'I think I'm still a little stunned.' She met his gaze steadily, her eyes unclouded, feeling as if a great weight had been lifted from her shoulders. 'But I've gone nowhere. I'm here with you, and that's the only place I want to be.' She reached up and kissed him on the cheek. 'Andreas *mou*,' she added, her lips trembling into a smile. 'See, I'm learning Greek.'

He pulled her against him, making her burningly aware of his need for her. 'And I cannot wait to become your teacher,' he muttered roughly into her hair.

'Must we—wait?' She whispered the words against his skin.

'Yes,' he said. 'And yes, again, for all the reasons I have already given and a hundred more.' He put her away from him, his mouth twisting ruefully. 'Which is why I think we should continue our tour as soon as we're dry—find somewhere with other people, *pedhi mou*. Where my self-control will not be under such strain.'

Her smile became mischievous. 'I think that comes with the territory.' She paused. 'So where is there less temptation?'

'I can't think of a single place,' Andreas admitted unevenly, after a pause. 'But the Silver Caves are public enough, and have tourists. We'll go there.'

'Yes,' she said. 'It might be best.'

'Ah,' he said softly. 'My lovely girl, do not look at me like that.'

Zoe was trembling as he drew her back into his arms. He whispered her name, looking deep into her eyes, then his lips came down on hers for the first time, exploring its contours with infinite gentleness, restraining any more passionate demand with iron control.

And she wanted more—wanted it so badly that it was anguish to remain passive in his embrace. She needed to twine her arms round his neck, part her lips for the intimate invasion of his tongue, let her hands caress the long, hard lines of his back. Then pull him down to the sand, offering herself with unresisting joy, knowing the delight of his body naked against hers at last.

She was melting—scalding with desire, pressing close to him with a little pleading murmur. Candidly testing the power of his restraint.

His breathing was ragged as he released her, the dark eyes glittering hotly, his hands lingering reluctantly on her skin, savouring its texture, the racing heat below its surface.

He said hoarsely, 'And now we go, *agapi mou*, and at once, or I cannot answer for the consequences.'

He turned away, reaching for his clothes, and Zoe, with an aching, silent sigh, realised she must do the same.

The entrance to the caves was narrow, half sandy track, half steps leading downwards, but there were plenty o guiding lights on the walls, which glimmered like mother-of-pearl in their glow.

At the bottom there was a tiny wooden jetty, where the rowing boats were moored. The silver gleam of the water had an otherworld quality that was almost eerie, and Zoe was quite glad to be part of a queue of sightseers, and not on her own.

She was still shaking inside from the memory of Andreas' kiss, her lips throbbing with heat, her entire body pulsing with the force of the emotions he had awakened in her.

Think about something else, she adjured herself as the woman guide launched into a commentary about the history of the caves and their discovery. But how was that possible when she was with the man she wanted with such desperation, her senses reacting almost frantically to the warmth of his body, the essential male scent of him?

When it was their turn, she sat beside Andreas in the bow, aware of little but his arm holding her lightly, while their boatman sent them skimming across the surface of the lake.

The power of the cave's echo was being demonstrated with gusto from the other boats, with screams of simulated terror, and sinister booming laughs reverberating round the walls.

'You know the legend?' Andreas murmured quietly in her ear, during an infrequent lull.

'Yes, I read about it. A little spooky for my taste.'

He smiled. 'You don't want to try it? To call my name and see if I will be true to you?'

'It's not necessary. Anyway, I'm not superstitious.' Zoe bent her head, and made a business of dabbling her fingers in the water. But not for long. 'God, it's like ice.' She snatched her hand back.

'Then I'll call to you instead.' He was clearly undeterred by her lukewarm response.

'No,' she said quickly, aware of a sudden, inexplicable unease. 'Don't, Andreas, please.'

His brows rose. 'You don't dare have your good faith tested, *pedhi mou*?'

'It's just a silly story,' she said. 'And, besides, there are all these people around.' She managed a laugh. 'I'd feel such a fool.'

'Then we will come back some evening, when we have the place to ourselves, and the cave will give us its blessing,' he said. 'As a man of Thania I must obey the tradition before I marry.'

Zoe started so violently that the boat rocked, and the boatman growled a warning.

She said breathlessly, 'You're talking about *marriage*?'

'Zoe *mou*,' he said patiently. 'Have you listened to anything I have said to you? I thought I had made it clear I want you to share my life, not just my bed.'

'Andreas.' Her face warmed frantically. She dropped her voice to a whisper. 'The boatman will hear you.'

'He speaks no English, and he knows better than to listen, or repeat what he has heard.' He paused. 'Why do you still doubt me, *pedhi mou*?'

She said slowly, 'Because it's all happening so fast.' She paused. 'And girls like me don't usually marry men in your position. You must know that.'

His mouth twisted. 'Ah, you think you're too good for me, perhaps? You could be right. See, I admit it.'

Her hands gripped together tightly in her lap. 'Oh, please be serious. I'm sure it can't be this simple—that you're expected to propose to someone suitable. Make a—a dynastic marriage.'

'It has been mentioned.' He shrugged. 'But I have always insisted that I would make my own choice, *matia mou*.' He smiled at her. 'And although I did not know it, I was waiting for you.'

'I don't think I altogether believe that.' Zoe's flush deep

ened, and her mouth curved almost shyly. 'But I like to hear you say it.'

'You still doubt me?' he asked reproachfully. 'Maybe I should ask the echo to judge me, after all.'

'No,' Zoe said vehemently, as he half turned towards the corner of the cave. 'Please, darling. Not now. We'll come back another time, as you said.'

He looked back at her, his brows lifting. He said gently, '*Pedhi mou*, it's just a legend. Why does it disturb you so much?'

She tried to laugh. 'I keep thinking—suppose we call each other's names, and there's only silence. I—I don't want to tempt providence.' She gave a slight shiver. 'And it's cold down here, too.'

'You wish to go?' She nodded jerkily, and he signalled to the boatman to take them back to the jetty.

They were quiet on the drive back to Livassi. Andreas was frowning slightly, his fingers tapping the wheel with a touch of impatience as he drove. Zoe stole glances at him, wondering what he was thinking. Could he already be having regrets about declaring himself so recklessly? she asked herself with an inward shiver.

When they drew up outside the hotel, she said with a catch in her voice, 'Will I see you tonight?'

'No, *pedhi mou*. I have things to do, and people to talk to, my father among them.' He paused. 'But I will see you in the morning. We will spend time at the Villa Danae together, and talk and make some plans. At what time shall I come for you?'

'I'll make my own way there.' She wrinkled her nose. 'After all, we don't want to cause any more gossip than necessary.'

'Soon,' he said, 'the whole world will know.' He took her hand and kissed it, his lips swift and sensuous against her fingers. 'Until tomorrow, *agapi mou*. Sleep well, and dream of me.'

As the Jeep pulled away Zoe stood on the hotel steps,

lifting a hand to wave him goodbye, and paused, the realisation that she didn't want him to go suddenly overwhelming her in a wave of utter desolation.

As if, she thought, her heart thudding, something were telling her that it was over. That it was the end of her happiness, and she would never see him again.

She called his name, wanting to summon him back, her voice high and frightened, but the Jeep was already gone, leaving just a wisp of exhaust fumes lingering in its wake.

And then, as she had dreaded, there was only silence.

CHAPTER EIGHT

ZOE was thankful that neither Stavros nor Sherry were in reception to witness her making such a fool of herself. In fact, there seemed to be no one around at all, suggesting that they were all in the kitchen getting the preparations for dinner under way.

'What did I think I was doing?' she asked herself, grimacing. 'Screaming like a banshee after a man, who couldn't possibly have heard me anyway.'

Because that was what had happened, and there was nothing more to it, so there was no need to feel so—so doomed.

'You're just being totally absurd,' she told herself as she walked through to the courtyard and sat down at a table.

Yet it was little wonder that she should be in such a state of turmoil. Her whole life seemed to have taken some quantum leap into the unknown, and she was still reeling from the effects.

Which was why she'd wanted Andreas to come back, she reasoned. She needed the reassurance of his physical presence—the caress in his voice as he called her his own—the strong shoulder for her to rest against. The long fingers clasping hers. And the sweet heart-pounding magic of his mouth possessing hers.

But instinct warned her that she would be unwise to cling too closely, or become too dependent on him. That he had a life totally outside her own experience, and responsibilities that she couldn't even begin to comprehend yet. And that there would be times when that life would take him away from her.

That was probably one of things he wanted to discuss

with her tomorrow. To spell out exactly what marriage to him would entail.

It wouldn't be easy, she knew, but she would cope. And she would stand beside him, rather than drag him back.

Part of her attraction for him, she suspected, was the fact that she earned her living, and lived and travelled alone. Quite a change, in all probability, from the spoiled, sheltered girls who were part of his own world.

Maybe, too, he still sensed there was something she was hiding from him, and found this intriguing.

But no longer, she decided with steely resolution. She knew now that she had to tell him everything. That it wasn't enough to tear up the paperwork and call it quits. Because that would not bury the past. And, unless she was completely honest with him, the gift of the Villa Danae to her mother would always be there in the back of her mind, hanging over their lives like a distant shadow.

And she wanted no shadows, she told herself, smiling. No secrets, either. Just their voices, united, echoing together down the years to come. And she'd been a fool not to trust the legend of the Caves of Silver.

'You want something?' She looked up with a start as a harsh voice intruded on her reverie, and, to her surprise, found Uncle Stavros standing beside the table.

'Oh—just some lemonade, please.' Sherry, she knew, made jugs of it, fresh and tangy with real fruit, each day and kept them in one of the kitchen refrigerators.

He grunted and went off, leaving Zoe wondering, not for the first time, just what she had done to upset him.

Well, now was her chance to find out, she decided as he returned with her tall glass of lemonade and set it down in front of her.

'I've seen you before, haven't I?' Zoe tried her most disarming smile on him—the one she kept for awkward parents. 'Up in the square the other day—and this morning.'

He gave a jerk of the head in ungracious acknowledgement, and turned to leave.

'Excuse me.' Zoe was inspired by her new-found confidence. After all, she was going to marry Andreas Dragos. 'But is something wrong?'

'*Ne.*' He swung back to her, the heavy brows drawn together angrily. 'You, *thespinis*, you are wrong. You should not have come here, and it is best you leave soon, before more trouble is made.'

If he'd slapped her, she could hardly have been more shocked.

She said, 'I—I don't know what you're talking about.'

'You think I do not remember—I—Stavros?' He smote himself on the chest. 'You thought I would not see her in you, the child of the little Gina?'

Zoe said very carefully, 'If you're talking about my mother, I know that she stayed here once, a long time ago.'

'Yes,' he said harshly. 'She and that other one, her sister.'

Zoe blinked. 'You're saying that Aunt Megan—came here—to Thania, too?' She shook her head. 'I—I didn't know.'

'There is much that you do not know.' He paused. 'Go, *thespinis*. Go before more harm is done. More sorrow caused.' He leaned down towards her, his face forbidding. 'Andreas Dragos is not for you.'

She gasped, hot colour pouring into her face. 'I think that's my business—and his. You can't say that.'

'It is said.' For a fleeting second, Zoe thought she saw a glimmer of compassion in the fierce eyes. 'Now, the matter is closed. Finished.'

He turned and stumped away, leaving Zoe staring after him, too stunned to challenge him further.

Her throat was dry and burning, but when she tried to pick up her glass of lemonade her hand was shaking so much that the liquid splashed onto the table. And the sharp scent of the lemons was suddenly acrid—nauseating.

She leaned back in her chair, heart pounding as she struggled for self-command.

She had not been too overwhelmed by unexpected happiness to realise that her relationship with Andreas might not meet with universal rejoicing. That there would be those who would think she was not a worthy wife for him and who would not scruple to say so.

And reason suggested that there might well be serious opposition from Andreas' family, and from his father in particular.

But she had not expected such a direct and personal attack from someone who was not even a member of the Dragos clan. She wasn't even sure whether she was being warned—or threatened.

Her immediate thought was—Andreas. She had to see him—tell him what had happened. Needed him to comfort her—to assure her that she had nothing to fear.

But it occurred to her, suddenly and shockingly, that she didn't actually know how to find him. She presumed that he was living at the Dragos residence, but even that was not certain. Nor did she know where it was, she thought, swallowing. This was the man who wanted to marry her yet she didn't even have his address or telephone number.

She felt the same sense of unease as she'd experienced just ten minutes earlier when his Jeep had pulled away. The same desolate conviction that he'd gone from her life, and nothing would ever be the same again.

Which was ludicrous, she reminded herself forcefully. Because she was seeing him tomorrow morning at the Villa Danae, and then she'd be able to tell him everything. Pour out her heart, and all the doubts and fears that were pressing on her.

He'd told her to trust him, and she would have to do so. Trust him to fight for her, and their future. Because anything else was unthinkable.

She went up to her room, and showered and changed into a sleeveless dress in blue chambray, trying to banish the taut, anxious face she saw in the mirror with blusher and eye-shadow, but, all the same, not convinced she had succeeded.

She rinsed out her bikini, and went to hang it on the balcony rail. As she did so she heard the loud throb of an engine overhead, and, looking up, she saw a helicopter swinging low over the port before heading out to sea.

She put her hands over her ears to block out the sound. It seemed too noisy—almost alien, in fact, for such a small island. But, no doubt, it was simply passing over on its way to somewhere else, she thought, glad when the whirr of the rotors faded, and peace returned.

Most of the guests were already eating when Zoe returned to the courtyard. She glanced around her, only realising when her heart lurched in disappointment how much she had been hoping that, in spite of everything, Andreas would have decided that he could not stay away after all. That he would be there, waiting for her. And that she'd delayed her own arrival for that very reason.

But the good news seemed to be that Uncle Stavros was not there either.

As she took her seat Sherry arrived with the menu, and a basket containing bread and cutlery.

Zoe gave her a determined smile. '*Kalispera.*'

The other girl nodded jerkily, and did not meet her eyes. 'The veal stew is good tonight.'

'Then I'll have that, please, and my usual red wine.' Zoe kept her tone equable, but her pulses were jumping.

When Sherry returned with the wine, and the usual bottle of water, Zoe put a detaining hand on her arm. 'Sherry,' she said in an undertone. 'What's going on?'

'You tell me. You're the one dating the heir to the Dragos millions, as I guess you know by now.' Sherry positioned herself so that her back was turned to the rest of the courtyard. Her voice was low and worried. 'For God's sake, Zoe, have you any idea what you're getting into?'

'I've fallen in love,' Zoe said quietly and simply.

'Then you'd better fall out again, and pretty damn quick,' Sherry said tersely. She paused, her tone becoming almost pleading. 'Let me call your company rep on Kefalonia— get you a swift transfer out of here, before you get your heart broken.'

'You're so sure that will happen?' Zoe bit her lip. 'Suppose Andreas loves me, too. What then?'

'He won't be allowed to.' There was an awful finality in Sherry's voice. 'I don't know what's going on, but I've gathered that much at least, and it's not good.' She shook her head. 'Hell, Zoe, you don't know the power these people have—men like Steve Dragos. And believe me, you don't want to know. Just put the whole thing down to experience, and get out, while the going's good.'

Her face was suddenly wan. 'Even I've come in for some stick. Stavros's uncle was here earlier, shouting at him for accepting your reservation, and saying he should throw you out. Telling him that all English women are nothing but trouble, and that he was a fool to have married one. And he's always been so sweet to me before,' she added unhappily.

'Oh, Sherry, I'm sorry. He had a go at me, too, earlier.' Zoe straightened her shoulders. 'But I will find out what's going on, I promise, and get Andreas to sort it all out.'

'If he can.' Sherry gave her a quick tight-lipped smile and went off.

Zoe ate her meal without appetite that evening. Her instinct told her not to wait until the next day, but find Andreas tonight. Let him deal with the problems that seemed to be mounting up like thunderclouds, before the threatened storm broke and swept them away.

On the other hand, she didn't want to panic unnecessarily either.

She would have liked another word with Sherry, but it was clear that the other girl was keeping out of the way, and Zoe could not blame her. She decided to make things easier by opting for an early night.

She undressed, put on her nightgown, and lay on top of the bed trying to read, but she was unable to concentrate. The room felt stifling, but there was a coldness deep inside her that she was unable to dispel.

She felt totally bewildered by the way everything in her life had changed so diametrically. Only a couple of hours before, she'd been happier than ever before, caught up in her own special fairy tale. Now, she seemed to be living through a waking nightmare, unable to make sense of anything that was happening to her.

Not one person wished her well, she realised, her throat tightening wretchedly, or thought that her relationship with Andreas stood any chance of survival.

And she had to know why. Was it just the disparity in their social standing—the fact that he was probably a millionaire many times over, and she was just a teacher? Or could it be the difference in nationalities?

Nothing she could think of was enough to provoke the strength of reaction that she'd encountered.

She switched off her lamp, and lay, her arms wrapped round her body, staring into the darkness.

Darling, she whispered silently. My darling. Wherever you are, think of me now. I need you so much—and I'm so scared.

It was going to be another scorching day, and Zoe was glad to reach the shelter of the olive groves.

For a moment, she regretted not bringing her bikini and towel. But she was here to talk, she reminded herself, not swim and sunbathe, so she was businesslike in a blue denim skirt, and a crisp short-sleeved white shirt. There would be plenty of time for leisure in the sun later—when everything was out in the open at last.

She'd brought the deed of gift with her, together with the documentation to prove who she was. He would probably be angry because she'd said nothing before, even though she'd had plenty of opportunity, but, she acknowl-edged, that was a risk she'd have to take.

If he really loves me, he'll forgive me, she told herself. And if he doesn't... Well, she wouldn't think about that possibility, she thought, shivering.

She'd assumed that Andreas would be there already, waiting for her. She went eagerly up the terrace steps, but it was completely deserted, and so was the beach.

He must be in the house, she decided. But when she tried the main door, it was locked. In fact, there was no access anywhere, she discovered as she did a complete circuit of the building. Everything was closed up and shuttered. As if it, too, had turned against her, she thought, then derided herself for her over-vivid imagination.

She couldn't even say Andreas was late, because they hadn't specified a time to meet. He obviously had a lot of stuff to catch up on, she told herself, with a shrug. After all, she had no real idea of his workload. It was one of the many discoveries about him she was going to make over the days—months—years ahead.

He'll be here, she told herself. All I have to do is be patient—and wait a little.

She found a patch of shade, and sat down in it, stretching her legs in front of her, and fanning herself with her hat.

She took the papers out of her bag, and checked them through. She'd got copies of her birth certificate and her mother's will for verification purposes. And once she'd told him the truth about her purpose in coming to Thania, she would tear all the documents up in front of him. Relinquish all claim to the house.

She looked at her watch, and grimaced, then took out her ill-used book with renewed resolution. She couldn't just sit, straining her ears for the sound of his step, or every moment would drag like an hour.

But the next time she looked at her watch, she realised, startled, that an hour had indeed gone by. Before too long, she thought, we'll be running out of morning, and into afternoon.

She got to her feet, and stretched, then went to the edge of the terrace and stared down at the beach, her eyes searching the crescent of sand in case he'd arrived there by another route. But she was still quite alone.

She was conscious of a faint stirring of anger. For a man in love, this was pretty cavalier treatment. Well, she decided, she would give him another ten minutes.

But one ten minutes was soon followed by another, and eventually another hour had passed, still with no sign of him.

If she'd been scared the night before, she was frankly petrified now, and close to tears.

'Oh, where is he?' she asked herself. 'What's happened?'

She snatched up her bag, and walked back the way she had come, fighting her misery and uncertainty every step of the way.

Stavros was on the phone when she entered the hotel's reception area. She stood waiting for him to finish his call, and he rang off, giving her a wary look. 'Can I help you, *thespinis*?'

'I hope so.' She was proud of how composed she sounded. 'Can you tell me, please, how to get to Mr Dragos' house?' She lifted her chin. 'I need to see Andreas quite urgently.'

There was a silence, then he said, 'Andreas is not there, *thespinis*. He is in Athens. The helicopter came for him, and he left yesterday evening.'

She said huskily, 'He *left*? Without telling me? When he'd arranged to see me today? I don't believe it.'

Stavros looked more uncomfortable than ever. He said, 'He telephoned here before he went—and left a message for you. To say that he had been called away.'

'And you didn't think to give it to me?' Zoe's voice rose. 'What kind of a person are you? And what sort of hotel is this, withholding guests' messages like that? I actually went to meet him. I've been waiting all this time...'

'I did not wish to do it.' His voice was miserable. 'It was my uncle. He thought it would be better—kinder if you thought Kyrios Andreas had simply—gone. That you would believe he had chosen this way to end things between you, and you would leave in turn.'

'Then you're wrong,' she said. 'Because I know he would never do that. And how dare your uncle interfere in what doesn't concern him?'

'He meant it for the best, *thespinis*. He is fond of Kyrios Andreas—as if he were his own son.'

'And clearly he thinks I'm not good enough for him,' Zoe said curtly.

'I don't know, Kyria Zoe.' Stavros stared down at the polished counter in front of him. 'He says only that you and Kyrios Andreas cannot be together, but he will not give a reason.'

'Well, when Andreas returns, I intend to be here, waiting for him, however long it takes, and to hell with your uncle's disapproval.' She paused. 'Did the message say when he planned to come back?'

'No, *thespinis*. Just that he had been urgently called away.'

'Fine.' Zoe turned to go to her room. 'If any other messages come, please see that I get them at once,' she threw at him over her shoulder.

And heard him sigh. 'Yes, Kyria Zoe.'

But it was to be her sole moment of triumph, because there were no more messages. Three days limped silently by, and eventually her pride would not allow her to ask any more.

It seemed likely that Andreas would simply stay out of the way in Athens for the remainder of her holiday, thus avoiding any awkward moments or potentially distressing scenes.

But why did he do it? she asked herself over and over

again. Why pretend that he had fallen in love with me? Was it just some sick game to alleviate his boredom with island life?

If so, she thought, it must have given him a laugh a minute to see how easily she'd succumbed to his spell.

It was not easy to fill her days, but she managed it somehow. Succeeded, too, on the surface at any rate, in overcoming her sense of personal humiliation at having been dumped with such insulting ease. In spite of everything, she was not going to be driven away, she told herself with resolution.

She had braced herself too for a certain amount of covert amusement at her plight from the hotel. Instead she found herself treated with quiet friendliness.

She mentioned the subject only once to Sherry. 'I suppose everyone thinks I asked for this.'

'Nobody thinks that,' Sherry assured her, giving her a comforting pat on the shoulder. 'But I was always worried about you.' She hesitated. 'I know Andreas is gorgeous, but a hell of a lot of women have thought so, too.'

'Yes,' Zoe said quietly. 'I can imagine.'

Only she didn't want to imagine anything of the kind. It was too painful to have to admit she'd been just another item on a long list.

So, she hid her ever-present hurt and bewilderment somehow, and kept her smile in place, and her head high as she made herself join in some of the trips and activities organised by the tour company and the hotel itself.

At the same time, she was careful to avoid any of the places she'd visited with Andreas. The memory of that one, wonderful day when she'd believed herself loved was still too raw for that. His image was engraved on her mind, etched deep into her consciousness. Superimposed on everything she did by day. Coming between her and the mercy of sleep that she yearned for at night.

She could not handle any further reminders of him.

And she did not, under any circumstances, go back to the Villa Danae.

On the fifth day, she took a ferry trip to Kefalonia, exploring the shopping streets of the capital, and taking a short coach tour round the island's major beauty spots. And there were even brief moments when she found herself able to relax, and enjoy what she was seeing.

One day, I shall heal, she thought. I may even come back to Greece. But not yet.

It was early evening when her ferry docked. She came ashore slowly feeling tired, but almost tranquil.

There was a car parked directly outside the hotel entrance, and there were two men in dark glasses standing on the steps, talking to Stavros. Businessmen, by the look of their smart suits, Zoe noted casually. And the car was pretty glamorous, too.

As she approached all three men turned to look at her and she halted, their scrutiny awakening a sudden unease.

'Miss Lambert?' One man approached her, while the other opened the car's passenger door. He was smiling, and his English was perfect. 'My employer, Mr Dragos, would like you to join him for dinner tonight.'

Zoe's lips parted in a soundless gasp. She said icily. 'Please thank Andreas for me, and tell him I'm not accepting any invitations for the foreseeable future.' She paused, deciding to ignore the fact that a horrified Stavros was sending her frantic signals. 'I'm sure he'll understand,' she added with cutting emphasis.

'You are mistaken, Miss Lambert.' The smile was unchanged. 'It is Mr Stephanos Dragos, the father of Andreas who wishes you to dine with him. He is looking forward to meeting you, so—if you could come with us, please?'

'But I've been out all day,' Zoe protested, aware that she was being propelled courteously but inflexibly towards the car. She indicated the creases in her blue chambray dress 'I—I need to change.' *I also need to lock myself in my room and refuse to come out.*

'You look fine, Miss Lambert.' There was an implacable note in his voice. 'This is purely an informal occasion.'

'Are you just going to stand there, and let one of your guests be—hijacked like this?' Zoe sent her stormy appeal to Stavros.

'Mr Dragos wants to see you, Kyria Zoe.' He spread his hands helplessly. 'Also, he has a very good chef,' he added.

'Great,' Zoe said furiously as she was handed into the passenger seat.

'That, of course, makes all the difference. If I don't come back, don't hesitate to let my room,' she flung at him as a parting shot.

She sat beside the driver, quivering with temper, her hands clutching her bag so tightly that its strap cut into her flesh.

The road they took led past the Villa Danae, and continued to hug the coastline. Zoe had just given up trying to calculate how far they had travelled when the car turned down a side road, eventually coming to a halt outside a pair of imposing iron gates. The driver sounded his horn, and a security guard appeared as if from nowhere, and opened the gates for them to proceed.

As the gates clanged shut behind them Zoe felt her mouth go dry, and began to regret the jibe about not coming back. Sherry's comment about the power Steve Dragos could wield was another uncomfortable memory.

They were travelling along a drive now that wound through a large garden, with spreading lawns, and cypress trees. When the house came into view, she saw that it was much older than the Villa Danae, and probably twice the size, its pale walls festooned with flowering vines and other climbers.

There were several vehicles parked in front of the house, and Andreas' Jeep was among them. Zoe felt her throat muscles contract at the sight of it.

She thought, I can't go through with this. I can't...

But the car was stopping, and she was being helped out

and escorted towards the entrance. She halted, shaking off the officious hand holding her arm.

She said between her teeth, 'Kindly let go of me.'

It was cool inside the house. Steve Dragos had air conditioning that worked. Zoe hoisted her bag onto her shoulder, and buried her hands in the pockets of her dress to hide the fact that they were trembling.

A manservant in a pale grey linen jacket hurried to open double doors, and Zoe found herself in a spacious low-ceilinged room, furnished with sofas and armchairs grouped round a massive stone fireplace.

There was only one occupant. Andreas, tall in an immaculate dark suit, was standing, hands on hips, staring out of the window. Zoe checked at the sight of him, her heart hammering frantically.

He turned slowly and looked at her, his face unsmiling and set in lines of harsh weariness.

'Kalispera.' His voice seemed to come from a hundred miles away. He sounded like one polite stranger greeting another, she thought in swift anguish.

She lifted her chin. She said huskily, 'Why have you done this? Why have you had me brought here?'

'It was not my wish,' he said. 'But—my father's.' There was an odd hesitation in his voice. He paused, then added, 'He will not be long. He is resting after the flight from Athens.'

'Is that all you can say?' Her tone had a ragged edge. 'You don't think I deserve some explanation?' Her eyes met his in naked appeal, her pride splintering. 'You said—I thought you—cared for me...'

'I care,' he said quietly. 'Nothing can ever change that.'

She said, her voice little more than a whisper, 'And if I asked you to leave this house with me now—to go together to the Caves of Silver and call out our names to the echo—what would you say?'

He bent his head, almost defeatedly. 'I would say—no.'

She almost cried out with the pain of it, but forced herself to steady her voice. 'Did you ever—really want me?'

And saw him wince. He said, 'It no longer matters. Everything has changed. You must understand that.'

'I don't understand anything,' she said. 'Andreas, tell me, please—what's going on? Have you been told to give me up? Is that it?'

'I had no choice.'

'Everyone has a choice.' She went swiftly across the room to him. 'And I choose you.' She seized his hands, wanting to touch them with her lips, to place them on her breasts, but he pulled away almost violently. Stepped backwards from her, his dark face a mask of anguish, his breathing harsh.

He said, 'I cannot touch you, Zoe, and I cannot allow you to touch me. It is over.'

She heard the doors behind them open, and half turned.

A man was standing watching them. He was wearing dark trousers and a quilted crimson jacket, with a silk scarf folded at his throat, and his jutting brows were drawn together in a faint frown as he surveyed them. He was tall, with silver hair, and a strong, rugged face that had once been handsome.

Even across the room, Zoe could feel the aura of power that accompanied him. Sense the dark magnificence of his presence.

She thought almost inconsequentially, In forty years, Andreas will look like this—only I shall not see it.

When he spoke, his voice was deep, and a little hoarse, as if he was trying to suppress some emotion.

'So,' he said. 'You are Gina's child, come to me at last. Stavros was right. You are the image of her, *pedhi mou*. I would have known you anywhere.'

Zoe stiffened. She said coldly, 'I'm afraid that I can't return the compliment.' But she knew it wasn't true. Because every instinct was telling her that this was the man in the photograph that her mother had secretly treasured for all those years.

She glanced at Andreas, standing like a statue, his face deliberately expressionless. She thought suddenly, I don't want to be here. I want to put my hands over my ears—and run.

He said, 'Then let me introduce myself. My name is Stephanos Dragos—and I have the honour to be your father.'

'No.' Her voice cracked on the word. She turned on Andreas, face and voice fierce with shock and horror. 'Tell me it's not true.'

But the look of agony in his eyes gave her all the confirmation necessary. A look that she knew would stay with her until the end of her days. A look of knowledge and renunciation that said all hope was lost for ever. Consigning them both to private but separate hells.

And it was the last thing she saw as a pit of whirling darkness opened in front of her. She tried to say Andreas' name, but the darkness was all around her, consuming her, and she gave herself up to it.

CHAPTER NINE

SHE became aware of things. Softness beneath her. Light beyond her closed eyelids. Voices speaking quietly. Something cool, damp and infinitely comforting touching her face.

She forced her heavy eyes to open, staring around her in dazed incomprehension. She was lying on a bed in a lamplit room, and a man she had never seen before, someone with a thin, kind face and a small neat beard, was standing beside her.

He said, 'So you are with us again, Kyria Zoe. That is good.' His hand closed round her wrist, checking her pulse rate.

'Who are you?' Her voice was a thread.

'My name is Vanopolis. I am Mr Dragos' personal physician.'

Her mind stirred, beginning to collect images—memories. A voice saying impossible words. A man's eyes saying goodbye for ever.

She moved feebly. 'I feel sick.'

'Lie still,' he said. 'It will pass.'

'What—what happened?'

'You fainted,' he said. 'But fortunately Mr Dragos was able to catch you as you fell, so you were saved any physical injury.'

'Mr Dragos,' she echoed. 'But he was on the other side of the room.'

'I meant the younger Mr Dragos,' he said. 'Andreas—your brother. He brought you here.'

For a long moment, she stared up at him, absorbing what

he had said. Realising that it was not just a nightmare to be forgotten as the sun rose. And that her life was in ruins.

She thought, I wish I were dead.

She felt tears stinging on her face like drops of ice, and turned her head away so that he should not see her cry.

When she could speak normally, she said, 'I'd like to leave here now, please.'

'It is better that you remain,' he said. 'You have had a shock, and your father wishes you to stay under my care tonight. Your hotel has been informed.'

'And I have no say in the matter,' she said, with sudden fierceness. 'My whole life has been turned upside down. I don't even know who I am any more, and I can do nothing. Is that what you're telling me?'

He hesitated. 'I am sorry that you should have found out in such a way. I wished the news to be broken more gently.'

Zoe sat up, pushing her hair back from her face, feeling the room dip slightly, then steady. She said, 'It would have made no difference, Dr Vanopolis. There's no way such a thing could ever have been made acceptable.'

He sighed. 'Rest now, Kyria Zoe. Would you like some tea to be brought? Or food?'

'No,' she said. 'I want to talk to Andreas. Will you ask him to come here, please?'

He said gently, 'Perhaps it would be better for you to talk to Kyrios Stephanos first.'

'No.' Zoe thumped the mattress with her fist, her eyes blazing. 'Andreas. Or I swear I shall walk out of this house, and never come back, and to hell with your Kyrios Stephanos.'

He sighed again, but went to the door. Zoe lay back on the pillow. She still felt faintly nauseous, and her head ached, but her mind was clear. And for the first time she took a good look at her surroundings.

It was a large room, beautifully set out with highly polished if old-fashioned furniture. The bed she lay on was wide and comfortable, with a heavily embroidered coverlet.

The shutters were drawn, and in the light from the lamp on the night table she saw a book, lying open, face own, and a pair of discarded cuff-links. There was a leather suitcase in one corner, its contents spilling out onto the floor, and a man's jacket and tie were draped across the arm of a high-backed chair. A cupboard door was ajar, and she could see other male clothing hanging inside.

She felt her whole body begin to shake in frightened awareness.

The knock at the door was barely perceptible. Andreas came slowly into the room, remaining near the doorway, his face in shadow.

Zoe pulled herself upright, staring across at him, her eyes enormous in her pallid face.

She said huskily, 'This is your room, isn't it? Your bed. You brought me—here.' Her voice cracked and broke. 'Oh, God, Andreas, how cruel is that?'

He said with a terrible weariness, 'It was the nearest room, and you were ill. I—I did not think beyond that. Forgive me.'

She closed her eyes. 'What are we going to do?'

'There is nothing,' he said. 'I am my father's son. You are my father's daughter.' His voice was cool, remote, as if he had rehearsed the words so often that all feeling was gone from them. 'That is the only consideration.'

'When did you—know?'

'My father was telephoned in Athens by an old friend,' he said. 'Someone who had known about the original affair, because your mother was staying at his hotel when it began.'

'Stavros?'

'Yes,' he said. 'Stavros. As soon as he saw you, he realised who you were. And when he saw us together, he feared what the truth might be.' He shrugged. 'I suppose we should be—grateful to him.'

'Should we?' Her voice was low. 'I—I'm afraid I haven't reached that stage yet.'

'No.' There was a note of savagery in his tone. 'Nor have I.'

He moved forward. Pulled the high-backed chair forward and sat in it, still keeping a careful distance, impatiently pushing the discarded clothing onto the floor.

She heard herself say automatically, 'Andreas—your jacket. You'll ruin it...' and stopped, appalled, as she saw him flinch.

He said bleakly, 'You speak as if you were my wife, Zoe *mou*. Who is the cruel one now?'

'Oh, God.' She buried her face in her hands. 'I can't do this.' Her voice was stricken. 'I have to get out of here— go back to England.'

'No,' he said. 'I am the one who is leaving. I am returning to Athens tonight. You must stay, at least for a while. My father wishes to make the acquaintance of his daughter, and he has waited a long time to do so. Whatever your feelings, *pedhi mou*, you cannot deprive him of that.'

Her voice trembled. 'Did you know about my mother— about their relationship?'

'I thought I knew about all my father's women.' His face looked as if it had been sculpted from rock. 'My mother saw to that. ''I am dying and your father has a new whore.'' I lost count of the times she threw that at me when I was a child. But these were girls he kept in Paris, Rome and New York. Thania was his refuge. My mother hated it, and never came here. And on Thania there was no one, until he met her—your mother—and loved her.'

He paused. 'And after her, I think, no one—anywhere.'

He looked down at his hands, clenched tautly in his lap. 'My mother screamed that he was building a house on Thania for some foreign bitch.

'I can remember her laughing when it stayed empty, year after year. Laughing at the idea that this woman he loved so desperately would return to him one day, so that they could be happy together at last.'

'She was happy,' Zoe said chokingly. 'Happy with her

husband—my father. The man whose name is on my birth certificate, who brought me up, and looked after me. Why would he have done that for another man's child?'

'Perhaps, because he was a good man, and cared for her, too. She seems to have been a woman who could inspire love.'

Zoe's throat tightened. 'Yes,' she said. 'Yes, she was.' She drew a quivering breath. 'We were—a happy family. Or I thought we were.'

He said quietly, 'As my family, of course, was not.'

She said thickly, 'If your father was so in love with my mother—so endlessly devoted, why didn't he get a divorce and marry her?'

'He tried,' Andreas said quietly. 'But although my mother did not care about living with him as his wife, she liked the money and social position. She enjoyed her position as a patron of the arts—her high-profile work for various charities, when her health permitted, of course,' he added bitterly. 'My God, she used illness like a weapon. Even as a child I could see that.

'As his ex-wife, her status would have suffered, and she knew it. So, she became hysterical—threatened suicide. She had made an attempt once before, it seems, not altogether seriously, but my father could not take the risk.'

He paused, his face sombre. 'It was a hideous situation, and it affected your mother very badly. She felt torn between her love for my father, and the mounting problems that their liaison was causing. Because although she was willing to make a life with my father as his mistress, there was no certainty that my mother would have left them in peace.

'And in the end she could not risk it either, and—she left. She went back to England, and made him give a solemn promise that he would never follow.'

'Even though she was expecting his child?' Zoe demanded incredulously. 'He let her go?'

'Neither of them were aware then that she was pregnant,'

Andreas said quietly. 'And he did not simply—abandon her, *pedhi mou*. He could not have done that. He kept his word about following her, but he wrote to her constantly, pleading with her to return to him. He went on building the house for her, as a pledge for their future.

'And when she wrote back, telling him there was to be a child of their love, he was overjoyed. He replied instantly, begging her to come to him, sending an airline ticket—money. But they were returned unused, without explanation, and he had no further contact with her.'

Zoe gasped. 'And he just allowed that to happen?'

His mouth tightened. 'He had been seriously overworking—trying to compensate for the loss of his beloved woman—living on hope. This was a blow he had not expected, and as a result he suffered a kind of breakdown. He was ill for several months, and when he recovered his first act was to write to her, imploring her to reconsider. But all his letters were returned, unopened. Your mother had moved, and left no forwarding address. She seemed, indeed, to have disappeared without trace.

'And when, eventually, he tracked her down, she was already married, and he had the additional pain of knowing that she had called his child "Zoe", the name he had once told her he would choose if he had a daughter.'

He sighed. 'Even so, he wrote one last letter, telling her that he loved her still, and would wait for her always.'

He leaned back in the chair, his face tired and drawn. 'And I, Zoe *mou*, had to put my own feelings aside, and tell him, a sick man, that all hope was gone.'

'What did he say?' she asked huskily.

'For a while, nothing. Then he said that it was no surprise, because he had been grieving for her from the day she went from him. But that she had left him—you. And you had come to find him.'

Zoe shook her head. 'She never mentioned his name,' she said wearily. 'There was just—the picture. A painting

of a house she never even saw.' She spread her hands.
'How could she do that?'

'He sent her drawings—many photographs. And she
knew where it was to be built. Her imagination must have
supplied the rest.' His mouth twisted bitterly. 'Maybe she,
too, could not—completely—give up their dream.'

She said in a low voice, 'Instead, they destroyed ours.'

'You knew that he had given her the house,' he said.
'Why did you not tell me?'

'I was going to—that morning we were supposed to meet
there. I intended to hand back the papers,—tell you I
wanted no part of it, and that we should bury the past.' Her
laugh cracked in the middle. 'Oh, God, what a joke. What
a hellish, tragic joke.'

She paused. 'Did you never suspect who I was?'

'How could I—when I never knew you existed? My father always grew angry when I tried to discuss the Villa
Danae with him. He refused even to tell me the nationality
of his lover, let alone her identity. And my mother only
called her ''the foreigner''. The possibility of a child was
never mentioned. Then, that morning in Athens, he poured
out his heart to me—held nothing back. The phone call
from Stavros had alarmed him, of course. He realised he
had to put a stop to our relationship at once, so only frank-
ness would do.

'Even then, I did not believe him. God forgive me, I
thought it was a ploy to push me into another marriage he
could be planning for me. He had to show me photographs
of her—even that last letter before I could accept the truth.'

'She should have told me,' Zoe said numbly. 'Why
didn't she tell me?'

'Maybe she also wished to forget the past. Wanted you
to go on believing in your happy family.'

'Yes.' She wrapped her arms round her body, her face
anguished. 'Oh, why did I ever come here?' She bit her lip,
sending him a swift, remorseful glance. 'You knew, didn't
you, that I was hiding something?'

'Yes,' he said gently. 'But so was I, Zoe *mou*. I thought—I convinced myself that it was just part of the game of love that we had begun to play. And that, soon, we would have no secrets from each other.' He paused. 'And now, God help us both, it is true.'

'He was a married man,' she said with intense bitterness. 'He had no right to fall in love with her.'

'I do not think he had a choice, Zoe *mou*. No more than I had when I watched you coming down the stairs towards me, and all I could think was—"Here she is, at last."'

She bent her head, a solitary tear making its way down the curve of her cheek. 'Andreas—don't.'

'No.' He got to his feet. 'It will be better, I think, if we do not meet alone again.' He walked across and picked up his travel bag, thrusting his errant belongings back inside it, and zipping it shut. He turned and looked at her. 'We are fortunate, perhaps, that we do not have more to regret.'

'One kiss,' she said desolately. 'Oh, Andreas, God won't punish us for just one kiss.'

He paused at the door, his face haggard, his eyes burning into hers. 'No, *pedhi mou*?' The harsh mockery in his voice seared across her skin. 'I think we are being punished already—now, and every day for the rest of our lives.'

The door closed quietly, and he was gone.

A lifetime later, she heard the whine of a powerful engine, and the throb of propellers as the helicopter departed, taking him far away from her.

Zoe turned over, burying her face in the pillow he had slept on, and lay, unmoving, until the sound died away. She felt totally disorientated when she awoke the next morning.

Not long after Andreas' departure, the housekeeper had arrived and, tactfully ignoring her tear-stained face, had chivvied and coaxed her gently to another room in a different part of the house. It had come as no real surprise, either, to find that her luggage had been brought from the hotel, and unpacked. To see that her very ordinary nightdress had been fanned across the bed's sumptuous satin cover, or that an enticingly scented bath was being run for her by a maid.

What's the point of being a multimillionaire if you can't wave a magic wand when you need to? she had wondered with irony, realising she was being given an object lesson in how the other half lived.

Left alone, she'd walked over to the window, and drawn back the filmy drapes, staring out into the darkness. If only there were a magic wand to mend a broken heart, she'd thought, or wipe out memory, so that she could forget the smile in Andreas' eyes, and the warm strength of his body when he'd held her in his arms. And, most of all, the promise in his kiss.

A promise that could never be fulfilled, but which would haunt her for ever just the same.

'Kyria Zoe.' A tap on the door brought Dr Vanopolis. 'Your father is anxious about you.'

Her mouth curled. 'He's all heart.'

He said with slight reproof, 'He wishes you to know that he will not intrude on you tonight, but asks that he may see you in the morning, when you are rested, and calmer.'

'Rested?' Zoe challenged ironically. 'Calm?' She shook her head. 'Tell me, Doctor, are you licensed to perform frontal lobotomies?'

His faint frown held compassion as well as concern. 'Would you settle for a sleeping tablet instead? I will leave one on the night table for you to take after your bath.'

Thanks to the medication, she'd actually managed to sleep, but her dreams had been troubled and disjointed.

And now the night was over, and she had to face the day ahead. And the inevitable confrontation with the man who claimed to be her father.

She stared at herself in the mirror, trying to discern some faint vestige of Steve Dragos in her appearance. But as far as she could see, there was none.

I'm like my mother, and that's all there is to it, she thought.

The chambray dress had been removed, along with other items from the wardrobe, for laundering, so she settled for her denim skirt and a white top with short sleeves and a scooped neck.

After all, she wasn't out to impress anyone. She was a schoolteacher on holiday, and that was all.

The manservant from the night before was waiting at the foot of the stairs to conduct her into the dining room. Zoe took a deep breath, thrusting her hands into her skirt pockets, then walked in.

Stephanos Dragos was seated alone at the head of the large table, glancing through an array of international newspapers, but he pushed them aside and rose as soon as Zoe entered. He was wearing a shirt in Sea Island cotton, and a pair of cream linen trousers, and there was a vigour and determination about him that was almost tangible this morning.

A marked contrast to the grey-faced man who had destroyed her life with a few incredible words only a few hours ago, she thought.

'*Kalimera.*' He pulled out a chair, indicating that she should sit next to him.

She returned an unsmiling 'Good morning' and took a seat further down the table.

His brows rose slightly, but he made no comment. 'May I pour you some coffee? Or there is tea if you prefer it? And the rolls are freshly baked.' He signalled to the maid waiting by the massive sideboard to serve her.

'Just orange juice, please,' she said. 'And coffee. I'm not hungry.'

'But you must eat,' he said. 'Or you will make yourself ill.'

She looked back at him coolly, and levelly. 'Mr Dragos, I'm sick at heart already, and food will do nothing to cure that.'

There was a silence, then he spoke curtly in Greek to the maid who served Zoe, then scuttled out of the room.

Steve Dragos settled back in his chair, the dark eyes examining Zoe unblinkingly. He said, 'If you have everything you need, then we will talk.'

'There isn't a great deal to say.' Zoe drank some orange juice. 'You had an affair with my mother, and I was the result. I was happier not knowing about this. That covers it for me.'

'You have no curiosity about the past?'

'Once I did. That's why I came here, because I found the papers giving my mother the Villa Danae. I thought I needed to know about that, but I was wrong.'

'You speak of an affair,' Steve Dragos said, after a pause. 'But it was more than that. Your mother was the love of my life, and I lost her.'

Zoe put down her glass, her mouth curling. 'How history does tend to repeat itself.'

He was silent for a moment, then he said quietly, 'I thought there was little more I could learn about guilt or unhappiness, but I was wrong.

'I can make no excuse for loving your mother, little one. Nor can I apologise for it. Every word she spoke, every smile, every gesture was a blessing to my life.

'But, believe me, I never meant that hurt should come to you or to my Andreas.'

She looked down at the spotless linen cloth. 'In that case, you'll understand why I can't stay here. Why I need to go home.'

'This is your home.'

'No!' Zoe said in a stifled voice. 'It's not, and it never can be. That is—just not possible.'

'Not yet, perhaps,' he said. 'But one day you will feel it. Because my blood runs in your veins, *pedhi mou*.'

'Does it?' Zoe shook her head. 'If that was true, I'd feel it *here*.' She pressed a clenched fist to her breast. 'I'd be aware of some connection between us—but I don't...'

'I can be patient,' he said. 'I have learned to be. And one day you will accept me as your father.'

She flung her head back in open challenge. 'There are tests that can decide that, Mr Dragos.'

'You doubt me?' The heavy brows snapped together 'Then perhaps you will believe your own mother.'

He reached into the breast pocket of his shirt and extracted a sheet of paper, discoloured and fragile with folding.

Zoe took it reluctantly, and scanned the few faded lines There was no question it was Gina's writing, and it said simply that she was well, and happy and expecting his child. It ended with her love.

'And this was the last time she ever wrote to you?' She shook her head. 'It makes no sense.'

He said heavily, 'I have told myself the same a thousand times. And I blame myself, too. I should have gone to Britain, insisted that she come to me. But I had made her a promise, and, by some oversight, left no loophole,' he added cynically. 'So I could not follow without breaking my word, which she would not have forgiven.' He paused 'And the next I heard of her, she was married.'

He gave her a piercing stare. 'He was good to her, this man?'

'Yes, he was wonderful to us both.' She swallowed 'That's why I can't believe that he or my mother could have lied to me about something so important.'

He was silent for a moment. 'Did she never talk of me at all?' There was an odd note in his voice that Zoe recognised, shocked, as wistfulness.

'No.' She tried to speak more gently. 'I think she'd put that part of her life strictly behind her. But she kept your photograph, and she painted a wonderful picture of the house you built for her.'

'And which you have now inherited.'

'I came across the papers by accident, and wondered...

She swallowed. 'But the Villa Danae was never hers in any real sense. And it isn't mine either.'

He said quietly, 'But I wish you to have it, *pedhi mou*.' As she began to protest he lifted a silencing hand. 'Use it as you wish. Stay there sometimes. Sell it. Give it away. The choice is yours.'

'That's—very generous.'

'You are my daughter. I would give more, if you would allow it. Acknowledge our relationship publicly.'

'Oh, no.' Zoe bit her lip. 'It's too soon. I—I need time. I have to think about this—all the implications.' She looked at him. 'You must understand that.'

'I shall try.' He pushed his chair back and rose. 'Come, let us walk in the garden together.'

As they paced along the terrace he said quietly, 'Andreas did not have to tell me she had gone from me. I felt it a while ago.' He glanced at her. 'Does it hurt you when I speak of her?'

'No,' she said. 'How could it? We—we both loved her. I accept that at least.'

'Do you want to know how we met?' He sighed reminiscently. 'It was all because of a sprained ankle. I was driving back to this house, when I saw a young woman sitting at the side of the road, nursing her foot. I could see she was in pain, so I stopped the car and offered assistance. She did not wish to be taken to the clinic, so I brought her here, and my housekeeper bathed and bandaged her injury.'

'A romantic story.' Zoe forced a smile.

'But that was not your mother,' he said softly. 'It was her sister. I gathered she had hurt herself when she stormed off after some quarrel, not for the first time.'

'Nothing new there,' Zoe said before she could stop herself.

'No?' His mouth thinned slightly. 'I can believe it, although Gina was always loyal. I sent a message to Stavros at the hotel that his English guest was safe, and—Gina came to collect her.' He was silent for a moment, then said with difficulty, 'I loved her the moment I saw her. When she came into the room, she made the sunlight pale. And she confessed later it had been the same for her.

'I did not hide that I was married, but our feelings were too strong. We became lovers within days. I persuaded her to move here to this house, with her sister—to stay on with me here when the holiday was over. I could not believe such happiness existed.'

'Did Aunt Megan stay, too?'

'No.' That shadow crossed his face again. 'She went back,' he said shortly.

I'm surprised she didn't take the first plane out, Zoe thought, picturing her aunt's cold, self-righteous face.

She had a lot to think about when she was finally alone in her room that night. She was still determined to leave as soon as possible, but she couldn't pretend the day had been all bad.

In fact if she'd spent it as his daughter-in-law instead, she'd have enjoyed his company, she thought, sadness a raw ache inside her.

It had been established that she would call him 'Steve'. He objected to Mr Dragos, and she couldn't manage 'Papa'.

Maybe there would come a time when they could be friends, but accepting him as her father was beyond her. Even if she wanted a closer relationship, Andreas would always be between them, and she knew it.

She thought broodingly, I really need to get out of here. But that was not as simple as she'd hoped. Because Steve had no wish to see her go, and was swamping her with kindness. One morning at breakfast, she found a flat velvet case beside her plate, containing an exquisite string of matched pearls. And when she tried to demur, he told her shortly that they were a mere trifle.

In addition a car and driver were always at her disposal if there was anywhere she wanted to go.

He even suggested flying her to Paris or New York to buy a whole new wardrobe of clothes.

'I'm a teacher,' Zoe protested with finality. 'I don't need designer gear. There's nowhere I could go to wear it.'

And he sought her company constantly, and not just to talk about Gina. He wanted to know about Zoe herself— the steps she'd taken to achieve her career—her ultimate ambitions.

Whatever doubts she might still harbour, he was clearly convinced that she was indeed his long-lost daughter, and he wanted to know every last detail of the life she'd led away from him.

And when she said her holiday would soon be over, he applied charming but unremitting pressure on her to stay longer.

'You have made my convalescence a thing of joy, *pedhi mou*,' he told her, reminding her none too subtly of his recent heart attack.

And she couldn't deny she was tempted. It was pleasant to live in a beautiful house where the linen was changed each day by unseen hands. Where doors opened as if by magic as she approached. Where she was served delicious food that she hadn't had to prepare, and where her every whim was indulged as never before.

Not that she had many whims, she admitted silently. But she knew there was a whole queue of people waiting for her to develop some.

But fighting the temptation to go with the flow was the certain knowledge that Thania was no place in which to forget Andreas.

She dreamed of him each time she closed her eyes at night. Each time she turned a corner, or a door opened, she expected to see him there.

It was driving her mad. But back in her own environment, there was work to distract her, and a new job to apply for. A completely fresh start, she thought, and she would never need it more.

'I think I'll go into Livassi this morning,' she remarked

one breakfast time. 'Buy some souvenirs to take home with me—presents for people.'

She'd half expected Steve to enter some objection, but he gave her a preoccupied smile.

'A good idea, dear child. I have some matters of business to take care of this morning, but we will spend time together after lunch, *ne*?'

'Of course,' she said.

As they drove into Livassi she told Iorgos, her driver, to take her to the Hotel Stavros first.

After all, she'd been scooped out of the place without so much as a by your leave, and, although she was sure the hotel had been fully recompensed, she still felt she'd like to have a brief word with Sherry—offer some kind of explanation. Although finding something feasible would not be easy.

When Zoe walked into reception, she found Sherry behind the desk, her eyes on stalks.

'I don't believe it,' she breathed. 'I was going to take my courage in both hands and call you today. There's someone here, wanting to see you.'

For one sweet, painful moment, Zoe's heart lurched. Then she had herself under control again. 'For me? Are you sure?'

'He's having breakfast in the courtyard even as we speak, if you want to go out there.' Sherry leaned closer, lowering her voice. 'Is it really true—what Stavros' uncle has told him?'

Zoe sighed. 'Steve Dragos seems to think so, but for me the honest answer is I—don't know.' She shook her head. 'I don't feel I belong there.'

'And you truly had no idea when you arrived?'

'None,' Zoe said. 'Or I wouldn't have come.'

'Oh, come on,' Sherry said bluntly. 'Finding you're Steve Dragos' daughter is going to change your whole life.'

Zoe's smile splintered. 'It already has.'

'Oh, honey, I'm sorry.' Sherry patted her consolingly.

'But you must realise they'd never have let Andreas marry you anyway. He's well and truly spoken for. Her name's Tina Mandrassis, and her father is one of Steve Dragos' biggest shipping rivals. A serious merger is being planned, and not just at boardroom level, according to my Stavros.

'And she had this huge birthday party in Athens a couple of days ago, and there's a photo in yesterday's paper of them together, with her clinging to his arm. The caption said that the announcement of their engagement is expected at any moment.'

She gave Zoe a smile mingling anxiety and compassion. 'I'm sorry, love, but sometimes it's better to be prepared for things.'

'Yes,' Zoe said quietly. 'I'm sure you're right.'

But nothing, she thought as she turned away, *nothing* could prepare her for news like that. Oh, Andreas, how could you? she wept inside. Yet, to be fair, he was only doing the sensible—the expected thing, as she must do herself.

She walked into the courtyard, and stopped dead, her eyes widening in total incredulity, as she realised who was rising from his table to greet her with a sheepish grin.

'Hi, Zoe,' said George. 'It's really good to see you.'

CHAPTER TEN

'GEORGE,' said Zoe. 'What the hell are you doing here?'

Sherry had brought fresh coffee and left them to talk with a glance at George that suggested faint approval.

Someone available, in my league, and not a blood relation, Zoe mentally translated with bitter accuracy.

'I've come to take you home,' George said portentously. He produced a pair of airline tickets from his wallet with the air of a conjuror performing a difficult trick, then sat back as if awaiting applause.

'Have you gone mad?' Zoe stared at the tickets, then back at his pink face. 'George—I'm on holiday. That's what people do in the summer. And the tour company give you a return ticket.'

George fidgeted. He looked, Zoe thought with detachment, totally out of place in his crisp shirt and immaculately pressed shorts. What was more, a discreet glance under the table revealed he was wearing socks with his sandals.

'I know, Zoe,' he said. 'But your aunt Megan wasn't very happy about you coming here, and she insisted I bring you back. She even paid for the airfares.'

'Now I know you're crazy,' Zoe said flatly. 'Aunt Megan doesn't care if I live or die.'

'That's where you're wrong,' George said, pouring himself some more coffee. 'Because when I mentioned Thania, she became almost hysterical. My mother had to find the medicinal brandy.'

'You mentioned? How did you know where I was?' Zoe demanded.

George looked slightly abashed. 'Oh, I happened to be

156

chatting to Adele's sister at the travel agents' one day, and she told me where you'd gone.'

'You were checking up on me?' Zoe's voice rose. 'How dare you?'

'I wouldn't put it quite like that,' George returned defensively.

He produced a handkerchief, and dabbed at his forehead, casting a dubious look around him. 'It isn't quite as primitive as I expected,' he confided. 'But it wouldn't be my choice. I've never felt such heat.'

'Well, don't worry about it, George,' Zoe said crisply. 'You've got your ticket home. Use it. I'll leave when I'm ready, and it won't be at Aunt Megan's behest. She has some bloody nerve,' she added furiously.

George gave her an uneasy look. 'Look, Zoe, I dare not go home without you. She was saying the most dreadful things—claiming you'd get involved with some Greek chap.' His already flushed face went a deeper shade of pink, and he lowered his voice. 'That you'd end up in the most frightful mess. I've never seen her in such a state. Mother was quite shocked.'

'She must have been—to allow you to come all this way without a chaperon. But I'm afraid she'll have to get used to it.' Zoe pushed back her chair, and rose, anger simmering inside her. 'Because I've been invited to stay on for a while longer, and I'm seriously considering it. Have a nice day, George.'

'Oh, don't rush off.' He looked as if he'd been slapped. 'Not when I've come all this way to see you.' He gave her a look of entreaty. 'Have dinner with me tonight—please?'

Clearly, she was going to be wined, dined and talked around, Zoe thought caustically. But at the same time she felt a modicum of sympathy for George, trapped between those two harridans in England and her own displeasure, although, admittedly, he'd brought it on himself.

He desperately needed to develop some backbone, she thought. If it wasn't already too late.

'All right,' she capitulated reluctantly. 'I'll meet you here at eight. And now I must go.'

She had told Iorgos to meet her in the square, but once she had bought a piece of local pottery for Adele her shopping was complete, leaving her with time to kill.

She made her way to the *kafeneion* she'd used before and ordered a Coke. The backgammon players were already deeply engrossed under the trees, but she hardly gave them a glance. She was too preoccupied with George's extraordinary arrival, and the reasons behind it.

Clearly Aunt Megan was terrified that she would discover the truth about her parentage. That was the only explanation.

But she's never concerned herself about me before, she thought, slowly. So why start now?

Especially when the last thing she needed was another mystery.

She was counting out the money for her drink when a gruff voice said, *'Thespinis,'* and she looked up to see Uncle Stavros standing beside her.

'You have something else to say?' She could not keep the antagonism out of her voice, and he sighed.

'Just that I regret I have had to cause you unhappiness, Kyria Zoe.' He shook his head. 'So much wretchedness over so many years. When will it all end?' He paused. 'May I sit? Drink coffee with you?'

'If you wish.' Faintly bewildered, she watched him signal to the waiter.

When the tiny cups of dark fluid were set in front of them, he said, 'I wish to tell you, *thespinis*, that I was saddened to hear of your mother's death. She was a very wonderful young woman. Kind as well as beautiful.' He sighed again. 'Any man would have been proud to love her, and my friend Stephanos—he gave her his worship.'

'Yes,' Zoe said more gently. 'I think he did.'

'They should have been together. Yes, he was married

but his wife gave him nothing. Why did she not come back, *thespinis*?'

'Because she married, too. Made a life for herself.'

'Then I am wrong,' he said, half to himself. 'It was not because of that other one.'

Zoe put down her cup. 'Are you talking about my aunt Megan?'

'Pardon, *thespinis*. I do not mean to offend.'

'No,' she said. 'I—I need to know. They were on holiday together, weren't they?'

'Two beautiful girls, *po, po, po*.' He sighed gustily. 'But with the older one, the beauty was in the face, not in the heart. Underneath there was all this rage—this bitterness.'

'Even then?' Zoe shook her head. 'Why on earth did my mother decide to go away with her?'

'Perhaps, because she wished her sister to be happy. But every day there were quarrels. Many times I saw your mother fighting tears, and it made me angry also to see how she made allowances—how she forgave so many unforgivable things.'

His face was sombre. 'It was good when the woman, your aunt, went away. She had caused such problems, I feared what more might come.'

'But why?' Zoe stared at him. 'Why should she do such things?'

He leaned towards her, his voice low and fierce. 'Because she was jealous, Kyria Zoe. Because she too was in love with my friend Stephanos. And he never looked at her.'

It was a day for shocks, Zoe thought, staring out at the sea. She hadn't gone back to the house, because she knew she needed quiet and privacy in order to think. She'd remembered the taverna on the cliff where Andreas had once taken her for lunch, and had persuaded Iorgos to drive her there, instead.

He was in the bar, enjoying a cheerful conversation with

the owner, and eating *souvlaki*, while she sat alone, toying with some grilled fish and a glass of white wine, trying to come to terms with Uncle Stavros' revelations.

It was hard to visualise her harsh, vindictive aunt swept away by overwhelming passion. Yet, she recalled, Steve Dragos had met her first—rescued her, in fact, and taken her to his house. Had Megan read too much into a simple act of kindness—of *philoxenia*, the Greek love of the stranger?

And then he'd added insult to injury by falling in love with her younger sister—the girl who'd always had the ability to draw people to her.

Something the other sister clearly lacked.

And had she really carried that sense of injury for so many years?

Remembering her violent reaction to the painting, Zoe could well believe it, and found herself shivering.

But it did not explain why her aunt had gone to the extreme measure of dispatching George to bring her home. Unless it had something to do with the 'problems' to which Stavros had so darkly referred.

There must be something she doesn't want me to find out, even now, she thought. But what?

Some kind of confrontation with her aunt now seemed inevitable, however much she might shrink from the prospect. Although there was no guarantee, of course, that Mrs Arnold would tell her anything—least of all the truth.

I'll cross that bridge when I come to it, she shrugged mentally.

But this new twist had finally decided her not to delay her return after all, even though Steve would be disappointed.

Maybe when I know the whole truth, I'll be able to put it behind me, once and for all, and get some peace, she thought with more optimism than conviction.

On impulse, she got Iorgos to drive her round the island

one last time. To say goodbye, she thought. Because instinct told her that she might never come back.

She would sell the Villa Danae, and if Steve would not take the purchase price from her, then she would give it to charity.

She wanted it finished, she thought wearily. All ties severed.

And she would have to make it clear to Steve that when they met in the future, it would have to be on neutral territory.

When she arrived back at the house, Andoni, her father's major-domo was waiting for her, clearly excited about something. 'Kyrios Stephanos wishes to see you, *kyria*. He has been waiting.'

He was in the room he used as a study, seated behind his desk.

He rose as she entered. 'You have been gone a long time, *pedhi mou*. I was concerned.'

She shrugged. 'I decided to have lunch out, and do some sightseeing. Is there a problem?'

'Perhaps. Yes, I think so.' He looked longingly at the box of cigars on his desk, then averted his gaze. 'We have unexpected visitors, my child. I learned this morning that Petros Mandrassis was on his way to Thania to discuss the merger of our two lines. He has now arrived, and his daughter Christina is with him.'

He paused. 'Also Andreas,' he added flatly.

She was very still, staring past him with eyes that saw nothing.

She said, 'Then I'll move back to the hotel.'

'Unfortunately, *pedhi mou*, you must remain here.' Face and voice were implacable, reminding her suddenly that this was a man who gave orders and had them obeyed without question. 'I am sorry to insist, but I need your presence at dinner tonight.'

'But I'm dining in Livassi tonight.' She confronted him with assumed calm. 'An old friend's in town.'

'Then you must postpone this engagement.' She heard the authentic note of steel. 'Mandrassis dotes on his only child, and she has complained to him that she feels neglected, because Andreas has been here on Thania instead of paying court to her in Athens.'

His mouth tightened. 'Also he has heard—rumours of another attachment, and this has caused offence. As a result, the merger is in danger.

'I need to set his mind at rest to secure it. Therefore I wish you to attend the dinner party tonight, and allow me to introduce you as my daughter.'

'No,' Zoe flared at him. 'I'm just not ready for that—to be announced as your bastard to complete strangers.'

He winced. 'If there is shame, it should be attached to me, not you, *pedhi mou*.'

'And, anyway, you can't risk me being identified as Andreas' passing fancy.' Zoe lifted her chin. 'Well, I have another solution. May I invite a guest of my own tonight?'

'A man?' He frowned swiftly.

'Yes, as it happens, which should silence any lingering doubts about me.' She paused. 'He's on holiday, so he won't have a dinner jacket.'

'Then I will make it clear it is to be an informal occasion.' He thought for a moment. 'It could be an answer.' He glanced at her, his frown deepening. 'So who is this man? What is he to you?'

'A friend,' she said. 'And a colleague from work. Nothing more.'

'He would like it to be more, perhaps?' His dark eyes were shrewd, and he grunted with satisfaction at her reluctant nod.

'Perhaps,' she said.

'Then there is no need to emphasise the working relationship,' he ordained briskly. 'Telephone him, my child. Make the invitation.'

George, however, did not seem overwhelmed by his good fortune.

'I thought I was going to have you to myself,' he returned, a touch sulkily.

'Do this for me,' Zoe said levelly, 'and I'll reconsider flying back with you.' *In fact, given half a chance, I'd leave now.* 'Is it a deal?'

'Oh,' he said, cheering. 'In that case—OK.'

'Thanks, George, you're a treasure. I'll send a car to pick you up in a couple of hours.'

'You will?' He sounded startled. 'Zoe—who are these people?'

'Oh, just a couple of multimillionaires with their heirs and successors,' she said lightly. 'The usual crowd. See you later, George.'

And as he began to make choking sounds she rang off.

Later that evening, she found herself wishing she'd accepted Steve's offer to update her wardrobe. There was nothing on her hanging rail that could compete with a shipping heiress, she thought with disfavour as she took down her black dress. At least she had her pearls to add a much-needed touch of glamour.

Her hands were shaking so much, she could hardly apply the modicum of cosmetics that was all she ever used. But tonight, she needed all the camouflage she could get.

She blotted out the sleepless shadows with concealer, and smoothed blusher along her cheekbones. She darkened her lashes with mascara, and applied a soft pink lustre to her mouth.

She'd aimed to appear cool and sophisticated, but instead she looked scared and vulnerable, she realised with a pang as she took a last look in the mirror.

As she emerged from her room she walked straight into Steve, who was waiting outside.

'You look beautiful,' he said. He drew her arm firmly through his, and led her towards the stairs. 'I am a proud man tonight.'

She said huskily, 'I'm—not sure I can do this.'

'You are a brave girl,' he said. 'I believe in you. Now let us go down to greet our guests.'

But the only person waiting in the *saloni* was Andreas. He was standing by the open French windows, staring into the garden, an untouched glass of ouzo in his hand.

He swung round as they entered. 'Kyria Lambert.' His smile was crooked. 'I had not expected this pleasure.'

'Nor had I.' Her heart felt as if it were going to burst against her ribcage. She made herself smile somehow. 'How—how are you, Andreas?'

'Trying to take this merger to its conclusion,' he said. 'As I am sure you know.' He paused. 'My father tells me you have invited a guest of your own tonight.'

'Yes,' she said. 'I hope you have no objection.'

He drank some ouzo, watching her over the rim of the glass. 'How could I? After all, I have no right to object.'

There was the sound of voices from the hall, a girl's rich giggle. Andreas stiffened, muttering something that sounded like an obscenity under his breath, then swung back to resume his moody scrutiny of the garden.

Zoe realised with shock how desperately she wanted to take him in her arms, to draw his head against her breasts, and tell him that everything would be all right.

But I can't, she thought. And, anyway, it wouldn't be true. Not now, not ever.

And she swallowed, bracing herself mentally as Petros Mandrassis came into the room with his daughter. He was a fleshy man with small cold eyes, which he allowed to rove over Zoe's body, and she hated him on sight.

Christina was small, and petulantly pretty, with a mass of glossy dark hair, and a figure that already bordered on the voluptuous.

Give her a few years and she'll be fatter than her father, Zoe thought, pain prompting her to cruelty as the girl crossed the room to Andreas and slid her arm through his, looking up at him with a pouting smile.

'Petros, my friend.' Steve moved forward. 'Allow me to

resent Zoe Lambert, the daughter of an old friend, who is onouring me with her company for a few days.'

Petros Mandrassis spoke in a grating voice. 'I am harmed, *thespinis*.'

His daughter murmured something in her own language o Andreas, and laughed. He inclined his head courteously, ut his face was a mask of ice.

Zoe took the drink she was handed and stood holding it, s if she were clinging to some wreckage. She was thankful o her heart when the double doors opened again to admit George.

He was wearing chinos, and a shirt that just failed to be asual, and carrying a sports jacket over his arm. He looked ot and uncomfortable, and as if he would rather be anywhere than here.

Zoe went to him quickly, reaching up and kissing him riefly on the lips. 'Darling,' she said. 'It's so lovely that ou're here.'

She added in an intimate murmur that could be heard all ound the room. 'Remember that question you asked me a ittle while ago, before I came to Greece? Well, I've had ime to think, and I know that I'm ready to answer it now. o, when we're alone, you can ask me again.'

'Gosh, Zoe.' He turned brick-red, his face a picture of stonishment and pleasure. 'It's true what they say about bsence, eh?'

She took his hand and led him round the room, introlucing him to everyone in turn, smiling with a radiance hat made her facial muscles ache. Not looking at Andreas s the two men shook hands with the usual polite murmurs.

'It seems I am to wish you joy,' Andreas said softly.

'Looks like it,' said George. 'You could knock me down vith a feather, actually. I never thought I'd talk her round.'

Andreas smiled charmingly. 'Clearly you know all the ight words to say.' He looked at Zoe, and it was like being eared with a cold flame. 'You must be sure to invite me o the wedding. When is it to be?'

'Well, we haven't quite got to that—' George began, b‍
Zoe cut in quickly.

'I thought next Easter,' she said. 'And it's kind of yo‍
to take such an interest, *kyrie*, but I'm sure you'll be f‍
too busy with your own arrangements to bother with mine‍

'Oh, I think I shall be married long before that.' Andrea‍
still held her gaze with his.

'Terrific,' she said. 'I've never seen a more perfect cou‍
ple.' She turned to George, treating him to another burst ‍
radiance. 'Darling, you need a drink.' And she whisked hi‍
away.

'Arrogant-looking devil,' George muttered in an unde‍
tone. 'Don't think I'd want him as a friend.'

'Well, don't worry on that score,' Zoe advised hi‍
shortly. 'Do you want ouzo, or white wine?'

'Is ouzo that cloudy stuff that tastes of aniseed.' H‍
pulled a face. 'I'd better stick to wine.'

He began a catalogue of small grumbles about his Gree‍
experiences, from the smell of the drain he'd encountere‍
by the harbour to his failure to raise the temperature of h‍
shower above tepid.

'You're not implying the two are connected in som‍
way.' Zoe tried to joke him out of it.

'God, I hope not.' He sounded horrified. 'Do you thin‍
I should mention it to that Sherry person? She's married ‍
a Greek, you know, although he seems quite pleasant.'

'Yes,' she said a touch wearily. 'He is. And, no, Georg‍
I wouldn't say a word. After all, you'll soon be safely bac‍
in England.'

'That's true,' he said, brightening. He put an awkwa‍
arm round her and squeezed.

Zoe was thankful to her heart when Andoni announce‍
that dinner was served.

But to her horror she found she had been placed next ‍
Andreas, with a glowering Christina opposite. George, r‍
calling his company manners, applied himself to her pain‍
takingly, but either she did not speak English well enoug‍

to understand him, or considered him not worth her notice, because he received little response.

Zoe made two comments praising the food, to which Andreas acceded with cool civility, and then relapsed into silence. It was, she thought, safer that way.

But she could not escape the reality of his physical presence. She found herself terrified that his sleeve might brush her bare arm. That their hands might touch as they both reached for the salt or more bread.

She was trapped in a morass of small but potent fears.

When the leg of lamb that comprised the main course was served, conversation became general, and she was able to relax a little.

'I must say that it's wonderful to be somewhere with air-conditioning,' George announced buoyantly. 'My room was like an oven last night. I didn't bother with the coverlet at all, and I almost found my pyjamas too much.'

There was a silence, eventually broken by Andreas.

'Indeed,' he said, very gravely, and Zoe did not have to look at him to know that little devils were dancing in his eyes. 'You did not consider, maybe, taking them off?'

'Certainly not,' said George. 'Sleeping in pyjamas is much healthier.'

Andreas lounged back in his chair, eyelids drooping, a smile playing about his mouth. 'But also a little constricting,' he said silkily. 'Don't you find?'

George looked surprised. 'No,' he said. 'Not really.' And he began to eat his lamb.

As soon as conversation round the table restarted, and under cover of a noisy discussion between Steve and Petros Mandrassis, Zoe said quietly and fiercely, 'Stop it.'

'I did not start it.' Andreas, the picture of courtesy, poured more wine into her glass. 'Tell me, Zoe *mou*, do you honestly intend to marry that fool?'

'That is none of your business.'

'If so, take some advice,' he went on as if she had not

spoken. 'Leave George folded under the pillow, and sleep with his pyjamas. You will get more response that way.'

Her voice shook. 'You bastard.'

He laughed. 'Hardly an appropriate name—under the circumstances.'

She gasped. 'I—hate you.'

'You are wise,' he said harshly. 'I am trying very hard to do the same.' He saw Christina staring at them across the table, her eyes narrow with suspicion, and raised his glass to her in a smiling toast. She laughed back at him, apparently mollified, and he turned back to Zoe, offering her the dish of potatoes, every inch the attentive host.

He was still smiling, but the look in his eyes pierced her to the bone. He said very softly and evenly, 'There is not an hour of the day that I do not think of you, *matia mou*. Not a night that I do not dream you are in my arms, and wake in torment. I loathe myself for the feelings I still have for you, but I cannot drive them from my soul. I am in this—hell, and you are not with me.'

The quiet voice stopped. And in another second Andreas had joined in the conversation with the two older men.

While Zoe sat rigidly in her chair, pretending to eat, and praying for the evening to end.

CHAPTER ELEVEN

As THE plane circled above Heathrow George said, 'Zoe—are you serious about wanting to marry me?'

It was the question Zoe had been dreading all day. She'd expected him to ask it during the helicopter flight to Athens; while they were waiting at the airport for the upgrade to first class that Steve Dragos had arranged for them, and ever since the plane had taken off.

Maybe the champagne they'd been served had loosened his tongue at last.

She turned and looked at him with compunction. She said gently, 'Darling George, you know as well as I do that if I said ''Yes'' your mother would have talked you out of it within twenty-four hours.'

He sighed. 'I don't know why she's like that.'

Because she's a miserable, selfish witch, who's scared stiff of losing you.

Zoe thought it, but did not say it.

Aloud, she said, 'But there's one thing I'm sure of. One day you're going to meet someone, love her so much that nothing your mother says will make the slightest difference, and you'll walk off into the sunset together.'

'What about a sunset for you, Zoe?' He paused. 'It's him, isn't it? That arrogant Greek guy I met last night.'

'No,' she said. 'I thought so once—but not any more.'

'But it's hit you hard,' he said. 'I can tell. He was watching you almost all the time. So, why's he marrying Tina Whatsit?'

'Because she's got a shipping line,' Zoe said. 'And I have a degree in English. They're hardly comparable.' She paused. 'You didn't seem too happy when we were taking off at Athens, George. How are you about landing?'

'I'd rather not,' he said, losing some of his colour.

Zoe took his hand and held it until the plane was safely on the ground.

She thought, It's over. I'm home and safe. And I can teach myself to forget.

When dinner was over, they'd gone to the *saloni* for coffee, and Zoe had stayed close to Steve, reasoning it was the safest place to be. She'd wanted no more exchanges with Andreas, she'd told herself, digging her nails into the palms of her hands. She'd still been able to feel the reverberations along her nerve-endings from the last one.

She'd been afraid even to glance in his direction. She'd felt her skin warm with awareness each time she'd heard his voice.

George had left comparatively early, and she'd made a business of accompanying him to the door, and lifting her mouth for his awkward kiss. She'd gone to her own room shortly afterwards, pleading a headache, and encountering a coolly cynical glance from Andreas as she'd done so.

She'd been woken a couple of hours later by the sound of a low-voiced but furious row being conducted in the garden below her bedroom by Andreas and his father, and had realised she was thankful she didn't know what they were saying.

In the morning, Steve had proved unexpectedly amenable when she'd announced she would be leaving with George to catch the afternoon flight to London. In fact, he had done everything possible to smooth her departure, as if he'd recognised it was time for her to go. That it was better—safer that way.

She had not, however, seen Andreas, even to say goodbye, and didn't know whether she should feel glad or sorry.

'He has taken my Christina to see the famous Silver Caves,' Petros Mandrassis informed her, the small eyes glittering with satisfaction.

But would he call her name to the echo? Zoe wondered sadly.

The actual moment of leaving the house was unexpectedly emotional. Steve held her for a long time, then traced a cross upon her forehead.

He said, 'I will write to you, my child, and we will talk on the telephone, *ne*? And we shall see each other again, soon.' He paused. 'Not here, perhaps, but in Paris, maybe, or Rome?'

'Yes,' she said. 'I—I'd like that.' She forced a smile. 'Papa.'

And left him smiling.

She was unutterably weary when she finally reached her flat. She stepped over a pile of mail in the hall, most of it junk, tossed her case into a corner, and went into her tiny kitchen. She made herself some tea, opening a carton of long-life milk from the refrigerator, and carried it through to her bedroom. She took off her clothes, dropping them to the floor.

Tomorrow she would pick them up, and open her letters, and throw away dead flowers, and unpack.

But for now, she just needed to get into bed.

After the heat of Greece, there was a chill to the sheets, and she huddled them round her. She turned her head slightly, and looked up at her mother's picture, remembering the rustle of the dead bougainvillea under her feet as she'd climbed the steps, the sharp scent of the pelargoniums, and the ever-present whisper of the sea.

Maybe the picture was too harsh a reminder of all that she'd lost, and she should take it down. But tomorrow was soon enough to decide that, she thought, and was asleep before her tea had cooled sufficiently to drink.

She spent three days cleaning and tidying the flat, dealing with correspondence, doing the laundry, and shopping for food.

On the fourth day she took the pottery vase she'd bought

in Livassi and went to see Adele. The cottage next door was sold, and the new owners were already in residence, with fresh paintwork on the doors and window frames to prove it.

'You're back early,' Adele commented, making coffee, after the vase had been unwrapped and admired.

She set a beaker down in front of Zoe. 'I told you these small islands were too quiet. You should have tried Corfu.'

'Next time, perhaps,' Zoe said lightly.

'Did you get to see any of the places your mother saw?'

'I think it's all changed a lot since she was there—and Aunt Megan.' She paused. 'Have you seen her lately?'

'No, but they're all grumbling about her at the Garden Club. They say she was impossible at the last meeting— falling out with everyone.'

On the way home Zoe called at her aunt's house. She rang the bell, and knocked, but there was no reply, although she was convinced there was someone at home.

She must have known I'd come looking for her, and taken evasive action, Zoe thought as she turned away.

When she reached home she wrote a cheque for her share of the ticket her aunt had bought, and put it in an envelope with a brief note of thanks.

Two days later it was posted back, torn to pieces.

Steve wrote to say that he was missing her, and that there had been some rain. He telephoned, too, and she thought he sounded sad. She wondered if the date for Andreas' wedding had been fixed, but he did not mention it, and she could not bear to ask.

His lawyers in Athens sent documentation confirming that the Villa Danae now belonged to her, and she wrote back, asking them to place it on the market, and detailing what they should do with the money it fetched.

She bought educational journals, and studied the employment columns. She applied for several jobs in various parts of the country, and was interviewed for two of them. She was offered the second, a post in a city school with a headmaster who was battling successfully to move out of the doldrums, and up the league tables, and accepted it.

She found a renovated terrace house a few streets away from the school, and applied for a mortgage.

Everything was going according to plan—except that it all seemed to be happening at some great distance. Someone who looked like her, and spoke like her, was performing all these actions, but she herself was standing on the sidelines, observing and uninvolved.

The autumn term started, and she began to work out her notice. She and George ate their sandwiches together, and once a week went out for a drink after work.

'Mother doesn't seem to see so much of your aunt Megan these days,' he told her on one of these occasions. 'Not since she made that scene over you being in Thania.'

Zoe shrugged. 'I don't see her either. I've been to the house twice, but if she's there she won't answer the door. And Adele says she's resigned from nearly all the groups she belonged to. It's as if she's turning into a recluse.'

'I know the feeling,' he said glumly. 'I saw in the paper they're starting line-dancing classes. Do you think I should join?'

She grinned at him affectionately. 'Go for it, George,' she told him. 'What have you got to lose?'

By the end of September, the weather was colder, with high winds and heavy rain.

'Lousy forecast for the weekend,' the bus driver remarked as he pulled up at her stop on Friday afternoon.

Lousy weekend anyway, thought Zoe, her arms aching under the weight of the briefcase full of marking that she was carrying. She couldn't run because of it, and she was drenched and cross by the time she reached the flat.

She peeled off her wet mackintosh, and lit the gas fire before sitting down to look at the small pile of envelopes waiting for her. There was one with a Greek stamp, and she opened that first. It was from Steve's lawyers, stating there had been an offer of the full asking price for the Villa

Danae, and that, if it was acceptable to her, they would prepare the paperwork.

So, that was the end of that, she thought, and sat for a long time, staring at the steady blue flame of the fire, and hoping it had been bought by someone who would live in it and love it.

She was just about to start on preparations for her evening meal when the telephone rang.

'Miss Lambert?' It was not a voice she recognised. 'I'm sorry to bother you, but I'm a bit concerned about your aunt, Mrs Arnold, and I didn't know who else to speak to.'

'I don't understand,' Zoe said. 'Who are you?'

'My name's Ferris, and I clean for her. She always pays me on Fridays, only she was out this morning, and when I went back just now she didn't answer the door. And I know she's there because the drawing-room light's on, and the curtains aren't drawn—and, Miss Lambert, she's sitting there rocking herself back and forwards, and she looks ghastly. The place is a mess, too. There's things broken and even a chair pushed over.

'It made me feel really frightened. I thought of calling the police, and then I remembered you, and I don't think she's got anyone else.'

'No,' Zoe said. 'I don't think she has.' She thought for a moment. 'I'll get a cab, and come straight away, but there's no guarantee she'll let me in either. It may have to be the police.'

As soon as she got there she could see why plump, sensible Mrs Ferris had been so alarmed. Aunt Megan looked like a crazy woman, her hair all over the place, staring in front of her, her mouth open and moving as she rocked.

Everything seemed to be locked, but Zoe realised the key had been left on the inside of the conservatory door.

Oh, God, she thought as she picked up a stone and smashed a pane. Aunt Megan's pride and joy. She unlocked the door and went in, Mrs Ferris following uncertainly.

'Shall I come with you, miss?'

'No, I'll talk to her first. But if you could make some tea it would be good.'

She stopped at the drawing-room door, thinking that she would rather be anywhere but there, then tapped lightly and went in.

Aunt Megan was still in the same chair, hugging herself, and keening in a low voice.

Zoe went over to her, stepping over fragments of smashed porcelain and torn paper, and knelt beside the chair, avoiding a crumpled newspaper, and a big leather-covered book lying on the floor at Mrs Arnold's feet.

She said gently, 'Aunt Megan, it's Zoe. What's wrong? Has someone broken in?'

Her aunt turned her head slowly, and looked at her. 'Broken,' she said hoarsely. 'Yes—all broken, all those years ago. And never mended. And now it's too late.'

'I don't understand,' Zoe told her. 'Please tell me what's troubling you. I'd like to help.'

'No one—no one can help me. Because they've all gone now. I thought—one day—I would go back. I'd see him one last time. But the girl went instead, and I knew she'd tell him that I lied to him. And then he wouldn't want to see me.

'And I couldn't have that, because I always thought I'd be able to tell him—how I felt. Make him look at me as he used to look at her. And now it's too late. All too late.' She was crying, huge, slow tears that trickled down her face and dripped into her lap.

Zoe swallowed. She felt as if she were tiptoeing through a minefield. But she had to ask, just the same.

She said, 'Aunt Megan, do you mean Steve Dragos.'

'Stephanos!' The older woman glared at her, then subsided. 'Such a beautiful name, and he was so handsome too—like a Greek god. I'd hurt my ankle, you know, and he lifted me up, held me in his arms. I knew there and then that I wanted him to go on touching me for the rest of my life, but he never did so again.'

She looked down at Zoe. 'Because she came, and it was all different. He was still kind to me, but he only looked at her.'

She shook her head. 'She left him, you know, because he was a married man, and his wife wouldn't divorce him. I would never have left. I would have stayed with him always, if he'd asked me. I wouldn't have cared.'

She wrung her hands together. 'Why did he never ask? Why didn't he want me instead of her?

'And then she told me that she was going back to him, because she was having his child. And I thought of them together, making the baby, and I couldn't bear it. So I laughed, and said, ''Then that makes two of us.'' I told her that he'd been sleeping with me too all the time. That one woman would never be enough for him.'

Zoe said, 'And she—believed you?'

'I was her sister. Her older sister who took care of her. And he was a rich man, who was unfaithful to his wife. She knew there'd been others before her. I think she was secretly afraid that he wouldn't be able to stop his womanising, no matter how much he loved her.

'And I'd been ill with a tummy bug. I let her think I was sick because I was pregnant. Yes, she believed me, because I was confirming all her doubts, all her worst fears about him.

'I remember she said, ''I must think'' and she went away from me out of the house, into the street, and a car knocked her down. She wasn't badly hurt—just cuts and bruises— except for the baby, of course. Stephanos' baby.'

Zoe was scarcely breathing. 'You mean my mother had a—miscarriage?'

'She was weak,' said Megan Arnold. 'She let his baby die. If she'd been strong like me, a little accident like that would have made no difference. I would have given him children. I didn't care that they would have been bastards. But she cared. It was always the moral high ground with Gina. She blamed herself for loving him. She expected to be punished for it.' She smiled, suddenly, gloatingly. 'And I punished her.'

Zoe felt icy cold. Her teeth began to chatter. 'What did she say when she realised you weren't having a baby.'

'I told her it had been a mistake, but that next time I'd make sure.' She giggled almost girlishly. 'She believed that, too. Convinced herself that he wanted me more than her.' She shook her head. 'It made her quite ill. But she stopped reading his letters, even though he wrote and wrote to her. Not a word to me—just to her, although I pretended I got letters.

'She moved right away—got a job, and met someone else. Oh, he wasn't like Stephanos, but he loved her, and she knew she could trust him always, so she settled for that. And then she had you. The perfect little family, and I hated her for that.'

She sat upright. 'I went back to Thania. I saw Stephanos at his house. I told him that I'd always loved him. That I'd be anything he wanted—do anything that he wanted. I think I even went on my knees to him. But he took no notice. I don't think he even realised what I was saying. He just wanted to ask about—her. And about his baby.

'At first, I was going to tell him about the miscarriage, because I wanted to hurt him as he was hurting me. And then I realised that it would upset him far more to think he had a child that he would never be allowed to see. So I told him that Gina had a little girl, and she'd married someone else, so that his child would have a name. And that she never wanted to see him again.'

'How could you?' Zoe said slowly. 'How could you do those things—tell those lies—ruin two people's lives?'

'Because I saw him first,' said Megan Arnold. 'And he should have wanted me, not her.' She began to cry again. 'Everyone always wanted her. Even when I got married, my husband thought she was wonderful. And now he's gone, and so has she.'

She looked down at the crumpled newspaper, and moaned softly. 'And so has my Stephanos.'

Zoe's lips parted in a soundless gasp. 'What are you talking about?' she demanded hoarsely.

'He's dead,' the older woman said tonelessly. 'Very suddenly. A heart attack. I read it in the paper—in the business section. I was looking for the share prices, and I saw it. I've lost him for ever.'

Zoe spread out the paper, smoothing the creases with shaking hands. She found it almost at once. It was quite a long piece, beginning with his funeral, which had taken place in Athens the previous day, barely forty-eight hours after his death. It listed his commercial achievements, various philanthropic efforts he'd been associated with, and stated that the running of the Dragos companies would now be taken over by his only son, who had already taken control. It added that a proposed merger with the Mandrassis shipping line would soon be finalised.

As she shuffled the pages together she suddenly saw Andreas' face. It was superimposed above an item in the gossip column, briefly profiling the new head of the Dragos Corporation.

'Once a well-known jet-setter, Andreas Dragos has moved away from his playboy image over the past two years,' she read. 'His forthcoming marriage will no doubt provide him with additional stability.'

The door opened, and Mrs Ferris came in with a tray. 'The kettle's gone wrong. I had to boil a pan on the stove.' She gave Megan Arnold an anxious look. 'Is she all right? What happened?'

Zoe looked at the motionless figure. She said gently, 'She's had a bereavement.'

The doctor came, and then an ambulance, and Aunt Megan was taken off to a private hospital.

Zoe paid Mrs Ferris, and cleared up the mess in the drawing room. Then she sat down in another chair, and read both the newspaper pieces again.

I wish I could have been told, she thought sadly. I wish I hadn't had to hear about it third hand like this—especially like this.

Yet it all seemed to have been dealt with at phenomenal speed. He'd died, and two days later he'd been buried. Even if she'd known about his death, it was doubtful whether she could have made it in time. And did she have any right to be there anyway, under the circumstances? For one thing, she was probably the last person Christina Mandrassis would want to see.

Besides, journalists would have wanted to know who she was, and what connection she had with the deceased, so she couldn't blame Andreas for keeping her at a distance. In his shoes, she would probably have done the same.

And her instincts had been right all along, it seemed. She had liked Steve Dragos—could probably have grown to love him, but she'd always been convinced, in her heart, that she was not his child.

She folded the newspaper carefully, and slipped it into the big leather book for safe-keeping. As she opened it she realised that it wasn't a book, but an old-fashioned photograph album.

There were snaps from childhood and school-days, and there were lots of Gina, riding a bicycle, bathing in the sea, perched high in the branches of a tree, her face always glowing with happiness.

The look of a girl, thought Zoe, who trusts life. Who believes it won't let her down. A girl who would never think that the older sister who'd recorded all these happy moments could ever be the cause of her betrayal and heart-break.

She went on slowly turning the pages, until at last she reached the holiday in Thania. Her aunt had taken great trouble with these photographs, every one of them carefully named and also dated, she noted with irony.

If I'd only known the date of the holiday, she thought, it would have been clear proof that I couldn't possibly be

Steve Dragos' daughter. I was born at least eighteen months later.

And Andreas and I would have been free to love one another.

As it is, I'm alone—and he's about to embark on a marriage of economic convenience. And neither of us are going to be happy.

Sighing, she put the album away, and left the room to find a piece of cardboard to cover the hole in the conservatory door. Then she telephoned for another taxi and went home.

Some time in the distant past, she'd been planning an evening meal, she thought as she climbed the stairs to her flat. As she reached her landing she fumbled for the light switch, and the bulb came on, revealing a tall figure leaning against her door.

She clapped a hand over her mouth, stifling her scream, as Andreas detached himself and came towards her. He looked grey with fatigue, but the ghost of his old smile curved his mouth as he held out his arms to her.

'*Matia mou.*'

She said something incoherent that might have been his name, and flung herself forward.

He received her hungrily, and his mouth came down on hers. There was no gentleness in his kiss. No restraint either. The lips that parted hers were deeply and passionately sensual, and they demanded an equal response.

His hands parted the damp cling of the raincoat to find her breasts, stroking her nipples to exquisite arousal through the thin woollen shirt she was wearing, and she moaned her pleasure into his mouth, her entire body melting with her need.

When at last he raised his head, they were both breathless.

He said hoarsely, 'Your key, *agapi mou*, or I shall take you here.'

Somehow they unlocked the door, and stumbled inside, already shedding their clothes as they went.

When she was naked, Andreas lifted her onto the sofa, and knelt beside her, kissing her body, his mouth hot and urgent. His tongue lapped at her breasts, turning the enlarged peaks to flame.

At the same time, his hand was caressing her belly, moving down over her quivering thighs, and parting them. Her body arched under the exquisite intimacy of his touch, demanding more.

He was murmuring to her in his own language, his voice low and languorous, as his fingers continued their intense erotic play. She could feel the last vestiges of her control slipping away, and then suddenly her body imploded, consuming her totally with wave after wave of pure pleasure, so that she was gasping and laughing and crying out, all at the same time.

Andreas said her name huskily. She felt him strip off his remaining covering, then he lifted himself over her, and entered her, and she enfolded him rapturously, her whole body alight with the warmth and strength of him inside her, her hands clinging to his shoulders, her slender legs locked round his waist in total surrender.

It was a lovemaking born from a stark and compelling need, and Zoe answered every powerful thrust with passionate completeness, her body as wild and driven as his own.

Nothing in her limited experience had prepared her for this fierce glory. For the frantic necessity to take as well as give. For his mouth on hers, and the hot, sexual invasion of his tongue.

Deep within her, she sensed the inexorable build of delight beginning again, and felt her body quiver and shatter once more into a renewal of rapture.

And at the height of her pleasure, as she was overwhelmed by sensation, she heard him cry out in his own release.

Afterwards they found a wonderful peace together. Zoe took him to her bed, and held him in her arms while he slept. Later, she dozed, too, and he woke her with kisses and made love to her again, slowly and very gently, his body worshipping hers.

And finally, they talked, because there were things to be said, and questions to be answered. And the revelations of the evening to be discussed.

Eventually: 'So,' she said. 'When did you realise that we weren't brother and sister after all?'

'Not until you began the sale of the Villa Danae,' he said. 'And the lawyers showed me the copy of your birth certificate. I knew when your mother had lived on Thanis, and the dates did not match.'

'And yet you said nothing?' Zoe reared up indignantly. 'You let me go on thinking that we were lost to each other?'

Andreas pulled her back into his embrace. 'I did it for my father's sake,' he said gently. 'He wanted to believe it so much, *matia mou*. You were this wonderful gift that he'd waited for throughout the long years. That's why he wouldn't consider the medical tests that the lawyers recommended, because he refused to admit there was even a remote possibility that he could be mistaken. You were his beloved Gina's daughter, therefore you must be his, too. I—I could not take that away from him.'

He paused. 'The doctors had already told me that he could have another attack at any time, which would almost certainly be fatal. I wanted whatever time he had left to be happy. And he was, my honey girl. He thought of you—spoke of you often. Blame me for it, if you will.'

'No,' she said. 'I understand, and I'm glad. I remember the way he said goodbye to me. I think he knew he didn't have much time left.' She paused. 'I'm sorry I wasn't at his funeral.'

'It would not have been a good experience for you. Our funerals are very noisy, emotional affairs. I had to steel myself to endure all the aunts and cousins screaming and crying. Far better, *agapi mou*, to remember him as he was.' He paused. 'Your mother's letter was buried with him.'

'Thank you for that.' She kissed his shoulder. 'I think it was that letter that made him so sure I was his child—and Aunt Megan's lies, of course.'

Andreas' arms tightened round her protectively. 'That evil bitch.' His voice was almost murderous. 'She might have harmed you. You should not have had to face her on your own, *pedhi mou*.'

'I wanted to hate her,' Zoe said soberly. 'But in the end, I couldn't. She was just sad, and—hopeless. It made me see how dangerous love can be when it gets—twisted like that.'

There was a smile in his voice, 'And now you also know how good it can be.'

'Oh, yes.' She stretched herself against him, her smile widening as she felt his body's instant response.

'Zoe *mou*,' he said. 'Have a little mercy, or I may not survive until our wedding.'

She said, faltering a little, 'You're going to marry me? But how?'

'The usual way,' he said. 'With a church and a priest. And as quickly as possible,' he added, stroking her stomach. 'I wanted you too badly even to think of protection, so there could be consequences.'

'Don't you want us to have babies?'

'Yes,' he said. 'But I am selfish enough to want my wife all to myself for a while, too.'

'Andreas,' she said, after a pause. 'You—you don't have to marry me.'

She felt him tense. 'What nonsense is this?'

'You're engaged to Tina Mandrassis. The merger depends on you marrying her. I—I know that. So, I thought of the Villa Danae. My mother never lived there, but I could—if you wanted. And belong to you for as long as you wanted.'

'But you are selling the Villa Danae, *matia mou*, and the new owner would not allow such immorality under his roof.'

She lifted her chin and looked at him with suspicion. 'You seem to know a lot about him.'

He grinned at her. 'An entire lifetime,' he agreed lazily.

She gasped. 'You—*you* bought the Villa Danae. But why?'

'So that we could live there together. It needs people—children—love to bring it to life. I think we can do that. And I suggest we sell my father's house. It has few happy associations for me.'

'But what about the merger?' she demanded.

His hand began to caress her breasts. 'I am more interested in a different kind of merger,' he whispered.

'Darling,' she said. 'Be serious.'

'You think I'm not?' He captured her hand, and carried it to his body. 'But you obviously will not let the Mandrassis merger drop, so let me tell you what I told my father—that I intend to marry only for love. And I did not, and never could love Tina Mandrassis. And the only time I gave the idea of an arranged marriage any real thought was when I thought you were forbidden to me, and I was at my lowest ebb. I tried to tell myself that without you nothing mattered, but even that could not persuade me to marry for convenience. So, I decided I would remain single.'

'And celibate?' Zoe inquired dulcetly.

He grinned. 'I would have tried. But I don't think it is a condition that would suit either of us, my angel.

'As for the merger,' he went on. 'Mandrassis needs it more than I do, and I suspect he will proceed even without me as a son-in-law. And don't worry too much about the beautiful Tina. She inherited a lot of money from her mother, so she won't lack for offers.'

'And I'm bringing you nothing,' Zoe said wistfully.

His smile was wicked. 'You think not, *matia mou*.' His

hand strayed with delicate precision. 'I shall have to jog your memory.'

'I have total recall, thank you,' Zoe said severely, trying not to wriggle and failing miserably. She sighed. 'I didn't think it was possible to be so happy.'

Andreas bent his head and kissed her slowly and tenderly.

'And this is only the beginning,' he whispered. 'My love—and my wife.'

Modern Romance™
...seduction and
passion guaranteed

Tender Romance™
...love affairs that
last a lifetime

Medical Romance™
...medical drama
on the pulse

Historical Romance™
...rich, vivid and
passionate

Sensual Romance™
...sassy, sexy and
seductive

Blaze Romance™
...the temperature's
rising

27 new titles every month.

Live the emotion

MILLS & BOON®

MB

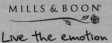

MILLS & BOON®

Live the emotion

Modern Romance™

IN THE SPANIARD'S BED by Helen Bianchin

Diego del Santo is dynamic, charismatic – and he's made millions. He believes everything is for sale. Cassandra Preston-Villers is heiress to an empire, beautiful and sophisticated – everything Diego has ever wanted in a woman. He blackmails her into becoming his – and their passion is explosive. But now Diego wants more…

MISTRESS BY AGREEMENT by Helen Brooks

From the moment tycoon Kingsley Ward walks into her office Rosie recognises the sexual invitation in his eyes. But she chose her career over her love-life long ago. Kingsley's initial purpose had been business – not pleasure. But Rosie is beautiful and – unbelievably! – seems immune to his charms. Kingsley decides he will pursue her…

THE LATIN LOVER'S SECRET CHILD by Jane Porter

Argentinian wine tycoon Lucio Cruz is not expecting the call that summons him to his estranged wife's bed. But Ana is suffering a partial loss of memory, and Lucio discovers that she's returned to being the fiery, affectionate girl with whom he once eloped. He knows he must resist her – in just a few weeks their divorce will be final…

THE UNCONVENTIONAL BRIDE by Lindsay Armstrong

Melinda Ethridge had agreed to a marriage of convenience to keep her family together. But she can't help feeling resentful about giving up her freedom. She decides the solution is to be an unconventional bride and retain her independence – including in the bedroom! But marriage to Etienne Hurst proves very different from what she expected…

On sale 5th September 2003

Available at most branches of WHSmith, Tesco, Martins, Borders, Eason, Sainsbury's and all good paperback bookshops.

0803/01a

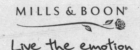

FREE!

4 Books
and a surprise gift!

We would like to take this opportunity to thank you for reading this Mills & Boon® book by offering you the chance to take FOUR more specially selected titles from the Modern Romance™ series absolutely FREE! We're also making this offer to introduce you to the benefits of the Reader Service™—

- ★ FREE home delivery
- ★ FREE gifts and competitions
- ★ FREE monthly Newsletter
- ★ Books available before they're in the shops
- ★ Exclusive Reader Service discount

Accepting these FREE books and gift places you under no obligation to buy; you may cancel at any time, even after receiving your free shipment. Simply complete your details below and return the entire page to the address below. *You don't even need a stamp!*

YES! Please send me 4 free Modern Romance books and a surprise gift. I understand that unless you hear from me, I will receive 6 superb new titles every month for just £2.60 each, postage and packing free. I am under no obligation to purchase any books and may cancel my subscription at any time. The free books and gift will be mine to keep in any case.

P3ZEF

Ms/Mrs/Miss/Mr ....Initials...........................
BLOCK CAPITALS PLEASE

Surname..

Address..

....

....Postcode ....

Send this whole page to:
UK: The Reader Service, FREEPOST CN81, Croydon, CR9 3WZ
EIRE: The Reader Service, PO Box 4546, Kilcock, County Kildare (stamp required)